The Grove Beneath the Ash

David A. Royster

Buaidh

Prologue

The wind played softly through the canopy, a spiraling hush of leaves and birdsong above a forest at peace. Sunlight dappled through the branches, painting the moss below in shifting greens and golds. High in the arms of a towering elder tree — sat Derwin. Bathed in the light of a cool spring sun, he sat. This young man did not look out towards the view that would stop a predator mid-hunt. Rather he lay slumped peacefully with his eyelids shut loosely — as if waiting for it to be described to him by the mountains themselves.

At eighteen, he carried the lean strength of someone who spent more time among branches and roots than walls. His long, dark hair — half-tied behind his head, the rest falling loose in the breeze — framed a face both calm and restless, one that always seemed to be listening to something no one else could hear. Barefoot, robed in earth-tones faded by sun and travel, he looked less like a teacher than an older brother who knew all the forest's secret paths.

A soft breath passed through his lips, not quite a sigh — not quite a prayer. Just the rhythm of someone at rest. Beneath him, the tree pulsed with life, roots stretching far beyond the unmarked borders of the grove, twined around stone and deep into cold water. He wasn't trying to listen — he didn't have to. The world spoke in a language he no longer had to translate.

"Derwin!"

The voice from below was young, impatient — a girl's, still soft with youth but sharpened with confidence.
He smiled without opening his eyes.

"Derwin, the lesson was supposed to start at third bell! You said if we were late again—" She broke off, suspicious. "I know you're up there!"

A leaf fluttered down past her head. Then another.

Derwin dropped from the branches like lightning, as if the branch was assisting in his ploy— caught a low bough, swung, flipped — and landed in a crouch behind her.

Ashling yelped, half fright, half laughter. At fourteen, she still carried the quick energy of childhood, but her gaze was sharp — the kind that caught details most missed. A riot of chestnut curls escaped the loose braid over her shoulder, and her simple tunic was streaked with soil from a morning spent anywhere but where she was supposed to be.

"You are so annoying!" she laughed.

He grinned, brushing bark off his robe. "Late again, Ashling?"

"I was only a little late. And you're a lot dramatic."

"Balance," Derwin said, tapping her gently on the forehead with his finger. "Nature punishes and forgives. But always remembers."

She rolled her eyes. "That sounds like something you made up."

"It is something I made up. But it's still true." He started walking toward the grove's teaching circle. "Come on. The roots won't wait."

They walked together through trees that leaned in like old friends. The teaching space was nothing more than a flattened circle of moss and stone, surrounded by small sitting stumps and woven leaf-canopies. A dozen other children were already gathered there, some cross-legged, some fidgeting with feathers or sticks.

Derwin stepped into the center. The hush came easily.

He knelt and scooped a pinch of rich soil into his hand.

“Every great forest,” he said, “was once something this small.” He held up the soil. “But even dirt listens. It remembers. And when you ask it kindly… it gives.”

He placed the soil down gently. Took a seed from a pouch at his waist — something round and striped, like a mix between a chestnut and an acorn. He pressed it into the dirt.

The children leaned forward.

Derwin did not chant. He did not glow. He simply placed his hand over the spot and whispered something only the earth could hear.

And the seed began to grow.

First a crack. Then a shimmer of green. A tendril, a sprout, a pair of tiny leaves curling open toward the sky.

A breath moved through the children like wind.

“That,” Derwin said softly, “is nature’s truth.”

Ashling knelt beside the sprout, watching the tiny leaves uncurl with wide eyes.

“Every time you do that,” she whispered, “it feels like the forest is watching.”

Derwin gave a small smile. "It is. But only because you're watching too."

"I don't understand."

"I mean," he said, scooping a second seed into her hand, "that the land only speaks to those who are quiet enough to hear it. You listen with more than your ears. That's rare."

She flushed and looked down.

"Now," he said, sitting cross-legged beside her, "try it."

Ashling placed the seed in the soil, hands trembling slightly. The other students gathered close.

Derwin watched her breathe, slow and steady. She placed her palm over the soil and closed her eyes.

For a moment, nothing.

Then… a tiny twitch. A shimmer. The soil cracked — and something green emerged.

It was small. Fragile. But alive.

The students gasped. Ashling's eyes shot open. "I did it?"

"You did," Derwin said softly. "But not alone."

He stood and addressed the rest. "The Circle does not give orders. It listens. Protects. Speaks when needed. All of you—"

He stopped. Something flickered at the edge of his senses.

The forest had shifted. Not in sound — in silence. A sudden

absence of birdsong. A tension in the leaves.

He masked it quickly, keeping his voice even. “All of you should practice with the seed spell tonight. Just once. Don’t push the land. It’s not your servant — it’s your partner.”

The students nodded, some already whispering excitedly as they dispersed. Most headed back toward the communal hall near the Heart Tree.

But Ashling lingered beside him.

“You felt that too, didn’t you?” she asked quietly.

Derwin’s eyes narrowed. “What do you mean?”

“The stillness. Like something held its breath.”

“You shouldn’t be able to notice that.”

“But I did.”

Derwin glanced toward the west, past the grove’s edge where cliffs dropped into mist. Beyond them lay the scarred valleys — the first places to rot when the blight came years ago. Even from here, the air seemed to carry their heaviness, like a breath held too long.

“Come,” he said, “walk with me.”

They moved along the forest’s outer ring, just the two of them. Evening poured gold and ember through the leaves, but the light felt thin here, the shadows too long.

Ashling skipped ahead, then slowed. “You’re worried.”

"I'm always worried," he said, though his voice lacked its usual ease.

She studied him. "It's about the druids who turned, isn't it? The ones who brought the blight."

Derwin stopped. "Where did you hear that?"

"I listen. The elders whisper about your parents, and about others who followed them. About what they did before they vanished. You're not like them."

"I hope not," he said, more bitterly than he meant.

"You're not afraid of danger," she said, "just of what happens if you stay too long in one place."

He looked away. "There are still dark hands moving out there. Old roots, hidden deep. If they find me… they'll use me to get to the grove. To all of you."

"Then fight them."

"I could," he said, "but the cost might be everything we have left."

Her fists clenched. "You always say you're a protector. Protectors stay."

He crouched, placing a hand on her shoulder. "Ashling, if I ever have to leave—"

"You'll come back," she cut in, fierce. "Promise me."

He hesitated, then whispered, "I promise."

A breeze moved through the trees — not the warm breath of the living forest, but something colder. Faint, bitter, it carried the memory of a smell he knew too well: damp earth soured by decay.

For a heartbeat, he was twelve again, standing beneath the Heart Tree as the first blight spread. The roots had curled like wounded animals. The wind had wailed through empty branches. And somewhere far away, someone he loved was already walking away.

The vision passed, but the scent lingered.

And for the first time in years, the grove felt less like a home… and more like a warning.

Chapter One

Three Years Later

The wind no longer spoke.

It slid through the trees like a ghost avoiding him, carrying no greeting, no song, no warmth.

Derwin moved in silence, boots pressing over roots he once coaxed from the soil. The path was still burned into his muscles, but the land had aged — scarred and hollow in ways that time alone could not explain.

Or maybe *he* had changed.

The grove rose ahead, and his chest tightened. The great Heart Tree — once the towering pulse of their lives — stood skeletal now, its vast branches crooked like the ribs of a long-dead giant. Pale bark flaked like dry skin, and the air hung heavy with the sour trace of old blight, faint but unforgotten.

He stopped at the threshold, one foot in the soil, one on the stone path. His staff — weathered and worn smooth by restless palms — felt heavier than it had the day he fled.

Derwin knelt, pressing a hand to the earth.

No warmth. No hum of recognition.

Not even the wary recoil the land once gave when it hurt.

Just nothing.

He looked up at the grove he'd abandoned. Guilt, grief, and

longing churned in his chest — but beneath them all, quiet and stubborn, a flicker of hope. That hope frightened him most of all.

The grove had not burned. Fire was too merciful for what happened here. The blight had no need for flame — it seeped and hollowed until only the shell of beauty remained.

Derwin stepped inside, boots scattering brittle leaves that once shone in spring gold. Moss no longer grew along the stones. The bloom-circle where they had held the Midsummer Rites was a tangle of thornweed and black-veined vine.

He didn't call out.

What was there to call to?

Instead, his feet followed old routes through the ruin, worn into his bones by years of lessons and starlit nights.

The teaching circle came first.

The sitting stumps were cracked and rotten. The leaf-canopy lay in a heap, its woven fronds rotted through. In the decaying remains of the field moss, small remnants clung stubbornly to the past — a carved spirit figurine, a braided grass ring, a length of colored twine children once tied around their wrists for luck.

Derwin knelt beside a bracelet of violet and green — the Circle's colors. His colors.

The knot was clumsy. Ashling had always tied them too loose.

He turned it over, tracing the single letter burned into the clasp: *A*

His breath left him like a long-forgotten sigh.

He slipped the bracelet into his pouch and rose, scanning the grove. The stillness here wasn't just abandonment — it was a pause. A hesitation. As though the land itself was deciding whether to mourn… or to wait.

The communal shelter was next.

It had not been destroyed in battle. The beams of living wood were pulled apart carefully, stacked in the underbrush. Gaps in the thicket marked old paths, deliberately covered. Even the hearth — now filled with leaves — had been swept clean before it was left cold.

Someone had survived. Not just survived — cared.

He pushed through a curtain of brush and found the old handprint tree.

Dozens of tiny palms still marked its gray bark, the tradition for every child when they first bonded with a spirit.

Beneath them, carved in the hesitant lines of a dull blade:

We waited. We watched. We had to go.

Derwin closed his eyes, palm pressed against the words.

Relief. Sorrow. Guilt. And that dangerous whisper of hope again, curling up from somewhere he'd tried to bury.

His fingers brushed the last word.

Go.

Where?

Why not wait longer?

Why hadn't he come sooner?

A sharp cry split the silence — not human. Not beast.

Derwin turned toward it on instinct. The voice of pain — low, gurgling, desperate. Something close. Something wounded.

Without hesitation, he moved.

The cry came again — low, guttural, and laced with agony.

Derwin sprinted toward the sound, heart pounding. Branches tore at his arms, roots clawed at his boots, but he didn't stop. The forest seemed to thin around him, leading him forward — or warning him.

He broke through a stand of bramble into a small clearing… and froze.

At the center lay a massive beast.

This monstrous beast bore the resemblance of a great elk and a dire bear — long-limbed and powerful, with heavy, bark-like fur and curling antlers grown from stone-gray bone. Its eyes were wide and wild, legs trembling as it tried to rise. A massive net — thick cords woven with iron rings — held it down.

Derwin felt the breath catch in his throat.

A rune-tethered snare. Hunters' work.

The creature shrieked again and thrashed. The cords sparked with sickly red light, driving pain into the beast's limbs. Blood stained the leaves beneath it — and not just from the trap. Arrows.

Two, embedded deep in its side.

"Easy," Derwin whispered, stepping forward, palms raised. "I'm not here to hurt you."

The beast bucked, eyes locking on him. It kicked out, and the net pulsed again, burning into its skin. The smell of seared fur filled the air.

He dropped his staff beside him and crouched low.

"I know it hurts," he said softly. "I know the ones who did this. You weren't meant to be here."

He reached into a pouch and pulled out a small clay vial. Healing salve. Not much.

He started forward — slow, deliberate.

Behind him, a branch cracked.

Derwin's body reacted before his thoughts did. He spun, snatching his staff up in one fluid motion just as a bolt fired from the trees. It missed his neck by inches, embedding into the soil.

A man stepped from the brush — armored in patched leathers, face hidden beneath a hood, crossbow reloaded already.

"You're not supposed to be here."

Derwin raised his staff. "Neither are you."

"Paid to track this one," the man said flatly, nodding toward the beast. "It's rare. Valuable. Meat'll feed a village. Bones fetch a fortune from bonecarvers."

"It's not meat," Derwin growled. "It's alive."

Another crossbowman stepped into view to his left. Then another. Three in total. Maybe more in the trees.

Derwin's heart pounded.

He turned back to the beast — it stared at him, one eye bloodshot, the other strangely calm.

Watching.

"Help me," Derwin whispered.

He didn't know if he was talking to the creature, the forest, or something deeper.

The nearest hunter raised his weapon.

Derwin lunged — not toward the man, but the trap.

He slammed his staff into the net's rune-knot. Magic sparked violently — pain shot through his arms, searing up into his shoulders — but the rune shattered.

The net collapsed.

The beast surged upward in a blur of hooves and fury.

One hunter screamed. Another loosed a bolt that went wild.

Derwin rolled sideways — not fast enough. A blade caught his side, ripping through his robe and into the flesh below. He hit the ground hard, breath stolen.

But the beast did not flee.

It turned.

It charged.

Antlers crashed into the nearest attacker, flinging him into the trees. Another tried to run — hooves struck like hammers.

The last hunter dropped his crossbow and vanished into the brush.

Derwin lay gasping on the earth, blood seeping from his ribs.

The beast stood over him, breathing hard. Its chest heaved. Blood still poured from its flank. It could have run. Should have.

But instead, it knelt.

Its enormous body lowered beside him, flank touching the dirt, head dipping to his level.

Derwin reached out a shaky hand.

The beast didn't flinch.

His palm touched the fur — warm, rough, trembling. But real.

A pulse ran through his fingertips.

Not magic. Not speech.

Recognition.

He let out a breath that was half a sob.

"Thank you," he whispered.

The creature huffed, then turned its head slightly — nudging his side.

It would carry him.

Derwin woke to the sound of birds.

For a moment, he thought it was a memory — the ghosts of an old morning long gone. But when he opened his eyes, he saw golden light trickling through pine branches above, the early call of thrushes echoing in the distance.

He was lying on moss, wrapped in thick leaves and animal fur. His robes were stiff with dried blood. His side burned. But he was alive.

And the beast was still there.

It stood just a few feet away, half-curled beneath a drooping tree, chewing absently on dry grass. One eye flicked toward him when he stirred, and it let out a low huff — not hostile, but alert.

Derwin sat up slowly, gritting his teeth. The wound had been dressed — not expertly, but carefully. His own herbs, he realized, pulled from his scattered pouches.

"You did this?" he rasped.

The beast blinked.

Derwin chuckled dryly and leaned back against a stone. "Of course you did."

They stayed there for two days.

The grove wasn't much — a tangle of trees and overgrowth half-swallowed by time — but it was familiar in its shape. Once, this had been a druidic outpost, a place of meditation and rest between sacred sites. Derwin recognized the old stone markers, the worn pattern of the moss ring beneath their feet.

He found an altar, cracked but unbroken, with faint carvings of sun, seed, and cycle.

Here, for the first time in years, he tried to listen again.

He sat at the altar each evening, pressing his palm to the stone, whispering not words, but intent. His magic didn't rise. The roots did not stir. But there was… something. A quiet presence. Like the forest was no longer turning
away, but waiting to see if he truly meant it.

On the third morning, Derwin stood.

His wound was still fresh, but it no longer throbbed with every breath.

He looked toward the beast, who rested beneath a patch of ferns.

"You saved my life," he said quietly. "You stayed."

The beast blinked. Then closed its eyes.

Derwin placed a hand on its shoulder — just for a moment. Then stepped back.

"I need to go alone," he said. "This isn't your burden."

The beast didn't move.

Derwin packed slowly, repacking herbs, adjusting his robes to hide the tear. His staff leaned against the altar, dry and cracked but still whole.

He turned to leave.

The beast remained, eyes closed. At peace.

Good, he told himself.

He walked eastward, through thick brush and morning dew, feet finding familiar paths. The guilt in his chest was quieter now — not gone, but settled.

He crossed a ridge of stone and was about to descend into the trees again when he froze.

Smoke.

A thin trail, curling into the sky — too far to smell, but fresh. Not wildfire. Not sacred incense.

A camp.

His hand tightened around his staff.

Without a word, he started moving.

The smoke faded from view as Derwin traveled, but its imprint lingered in his thoughts — like a memory refusing to settle.

He moved with purpose now, but not speed. His wound still flared when he climbed, and the roots beneath the forest floor had not quite forgiven him yet. Each step came with care. Each breath measured.

The beast followed in silence.

It never strayed far — ten paces behind at most, sometimes flanking him when the trees grew tight. When he stopped to rest, it stood sentinel. When he drank from the creek, it waited without impatience. When he stumbled — and he did, once or twice — it stepped in without a sound, letting him steady himself on its side without needing to ask.

Derwin didn't speak much. He wasn't sure what to say. Not to the creature. Not to the forest. Not to himself.

But the silence wasn't empty anymore.

He crossed through old trails partially reclaimed by nature — places he'd walked as a boy, paths where the Circle once led long seasonal journeys. Birds fluttered above, their songs no longer harsh with warning, but hesitant, curious.

In one clearing, he found a sapling bent in the shape of a crescent moon — a sign once used by traveling druids to mark safe passage. It was faint, overgrown, but still there.

Someone had passed through not long ago.

At dusk, he made camp beside a fallen cedar whose roots had formed a shallow arch, just wide enough to lie beneath.

The beast circled once, then laid nearby — curled like a mountain, breathing slow.

Derwin stared at the embers of his fire. He hadn't lit it for warmth. Just the light. The color.

He rubbed at the bracelet in his pouch — Ashling's knotwork, faded and worn. He hadn't meant to keep it, not really. But he hadn't let it go either.

"Where did you go?" he whispered into the flame.

The beast shifted slightly, lifting its head. One dark eye glinted in the light.

Derwin gave a tired smile.

"Don't tell me you understand all this."

The beast blinked. Then slowly lowered its head again.

The forest exhaled around them.

Morning came slow and golden.

Mist clung to the ground like forgotten breath, and dew glittered across every blade of grass. Derwin stirred beneath the cedar arch, groaning softly as stiff muscles protested his movements.

He sat up, rubbed his eyes, and looked to the horizon.

Beyond the rise of the ridge, just past the thinning line of trees… the smoke. Not the harsh black plumes of burning. These were soft and gray, drifting upward from stone-ringed hearths and hidden cookfires.

A settlement. Small. Cautious. Alive.

He stood slowly, letting the stiffness bleed out of his legs. The wound in his side had closed, though it ached in the cold. His robes hung unevenly — patched once with moss, now with beast-fur. His staff had cracked again during the climb yesterday, and he'd bound it in twine. It would do.

Behind him, the beast rose from its bed of leaves, stretching long limbs with a ripple of muscle beneath bark-rough fur. It padded toward him and stood at his side, shoulder to shoulder.

They both stared at the smoke.

Derwin exhaled. "So that's where you've led me."

The beast didn't answer. Of course it didn't.

But it stayed.

He looked over at it — this massive, half-wild creature that had dragged him from death, stood between him and a blade, and never once asked for a command.

"Well," he muttered, brushing hair from his face, "if you're going to keep following me like a loyal, moss-drenched hound…" he reached up, tapping his chin thoughtfully, "you'll need a name."

The beast's ear twitched.

Derwin grinned. "Don't give me that look. It's only fair."

He studied the creature for a moment — the rough, earthen fur, the eyes like weathered stone, the way it moved like it had been carved by the forest itself.

"How about…" he paused, "Stonefern? Barkhide? ...No, too dramatic."

The beast blinked slowly.

Derwin sighed. “You’re right. Naming things is harder than it used to be.” He stepped forward toward the ridge, the beast falling into step beside him. “We’ll figure it out,” he said softly. “Maybe once I figure myself out too.”

They walked together, the settlement ahead growing clearer with every step. Faint figures moved between tents and makeshift buildings. Small. Fragile. Alive.

Derwin reached for the bracelet in his pouch, fingers curling around it.

Ashling might be here.

If not, the trail had never been warmer.

He took a breath.

And he didn’t walk like someone searching for redemption anymore.

He walked like someone who would protect whatever he found.

CHAPTER TWO

The path wound like an old scar — half-healed and hidden beneath layers of moss and time. Derwin took each step slowly, leaning into his staff, letting the earth speak beneath his boots. It said little, but at least it no longer turned away from him.

The beast stayed at the forest's edge at the lift of Derwin's palm.

The settlement appeared through a veil of morning mist: a small ring of shelters nestled against a sloping hill, half-grown, half-built. Canvas tents patched with moss. Huts made from bent boughs and bark. A central firepit, long cooled, sat among it all like a silent witness.

No banners. No walls. Just survival.

Eyes found him before voices did.

A boy, no more than ten, dropped a bucket of creekwater at the sight of Derwin. Somewhere to the left, a mother pulled her child back into the shadows of a shelter. Others stopped mid-task — gathering herbs, weaving cord, hauling wood — all frozen in a moment they hadn't expected to come.

"Derwin?" someone whispered.

Then louder, "Derwin…"

The name spread like wind through dry leaves.

He paused at the edge of the camp.

He didn't speak. What was there to say?

He expected someone to curse him. To spit. To drive him away with blame or grief. Part of him wanted them to. Maybe then the ache in his chest would feel deserved.

A figure emerged from the central path — tall, broad-shouldered, with storm-gray eyes and a long braid streaked with silver.

“Joram,” Derwin said, his voice rough from disuse.

“You’re still alive,” Joram said flatly. “Thought you'd vanished with the rest of them.”

“I should have,” Derwin replied. “Would’ve been easier for everyone.”

Joram stepped closer. “Easier? Easier would’ve been if you’d stayed. If you’d fought.”

“I would’ve lost.”

“We all lost,” Joram snapped, voice rising. “The difference is we stayed to lose.”

More people stepped from tents, drawn by the voices.

“I didn’t come to justify myself,” Derwin said quietly. “I came because… something brought me here.”

“Guilt,” Joram muttered. “Or cowardice. Pick one.”

Before he could answer, a small voice rang out. “Derwin!”

It was a cry of joy, of disbelief.

From between two huts camc a blur of grccn and brown — a girl perhaps twelve or thirteen, with tangled curls and tears already streaking her dirt-smeared cheeks.

"Maelin," Derwin breathed — surprised by how small she still was, and how fiercely she collided into him, wrapping her arms around his waist.

"You came back," she sobbed. "I knew you would. I told them. I said you weren't gone."

He hesitated. His arms hovered for a moment — then folded gently around her, unsure who needed the hug more.

"You've grown," he said softly. "A little."

"You look terrible," she sniffled.

"I feel worse."

A quiet ripple passed through the watching crowd — not warmth, but something that wasn't quite rejection either. Not yet.

Joram looked like he might protest again, but an elder stepped beside him — shorter, older, but no less firm in presence. Her silver-threaded braids shimmered like riverwater.

"Enough," she said. Her voice was soft, but it bent the air around it.

"Mother Kesa," Derwin nodded with respect.

"You left," she said plainly.

"I did."

"We grieved."

“I know.”

She looked him over, eyes neither cruel nor kind. Just searching. “Yet you returned,” she said. “Carrying wounds. And a guardian.”

She turned her gaze to the beast, who still stood just at the edge of the woods, a towering figure amongst even the large forest greenery. A few children gasped, as they too now noticed the beast. One clutched her father’s leg.

The beast simply breathed and slowly began approaching Derwin's side as if on instinct.

“Is… is that your Echo?” asked a young boy, peeking out from behind a hut. His eyes were wide, but not fearful — only curious.

“My Echo?” Derwin asked, caught off guard.

“The spirit,” the boy said. “You know. The one the druids summon when they’re really strong. Like, really strong.”

Derwin blinked. Then shook his head. “No, nothing like that. Just a creature with very poor decision-making skills.”

The beast snorted behind him.

Maelin giggled.

“Still,” Derwin added, glancing up at the great antlered head as the beast met his side, “he keeps showing up. Dragged me out of a hunter’s trap. Watched over me for two nights. Even let me bleed all over his fur.”

He looked over the gathering crowd the older druids who remained, the wide-eyed children, the wary survivors standing between disbelief and memory.

Then he turned back to the beast and crouched slightly, voice just loud enough for all to hear.

“Well,” he murmured, “if you’re going to keep following me like some overgrown, moss-draped shadow…” he paused, thoughtful, “you’ll need a name.”

The beast tilted its head.

Derwin scratched at his beard. “And clearly I’m in no state to pick one.” He looked at the children — Maelin, the boy who spoke, the others beginning to gather behind her, whispering to one another. “Perhaps,” Derwin said, gesturing toward them, “they’ll help me find one.”

The beast blinked once, then sat on its haunches beside him, calm and unbothered.

Not a mount.

Not a pet.

A partner.

And for the first time in a long time, Derwin did not feel alone.

The settlement came alive as dusk rolled in.

A log fire was lit in the center of the circle, fed with dry wood and sweet-smelling herbs. Smoke curled into the sky in thin ribbons, carrying warmth through the cool night air. A cook-pot was slung over the flames, filled with root vegetables, forest herbs, and what little meat they had left. The scent made Derwin’s stomach growl for the first time in days.

It wasn't a feast. But it was enough.

And for a moment, as the firelight danced on children's faces and laughter rose from the youngest, it felt like home again.

The beast lay curled near the edge of the fire, resting but alert. Children crept close — cautiously at first — then braver by the minute. They whispered names to it: Mossfang, Oldbark, Thunderhoof, Sage. Derwin listened without comment, letting the game unfold.

Maelin clung to his side most of the night, her hands full of flatbread and half-roasted root slices. "You have to stay now," she said between bites. "They need you. We need you."

Derwin smiled faintly, but didn't answer.

Elder Kesa sat not far, sipping slowly from a carved cup, watching him with her ancient, unreadable gaze.

Some of the parents — especially those with younger children — nodded to him as they passed. One woman even clasped his shoulder in silence and whispered, "Thank you. For coming back."

But not everyone joined the fire.

A group of older druids stood near the edges of the clearing — shadows between tents. They spoke in low tones, casting glances that never quite reached Derwin's eyes. One of them, a gaunt man with a scar across his throat, didn't even try to whisper. "Wouldn't be surprised if he sold us out to save himself."

Derwin froze.

Another voice replied — one he didn't recognize. "That's why he lived when so many didn't. Made a deal. Ran while the rest burned."

He didn't turn to face them. He didn't move at all.

But their words settled like stones in his chest.

He drifted from the fire a short while later, under the pretense of needing air.

The night was cool and quiet. The stars above shimmered through branches not yet overtaken by blight or frost. The sound of laughter still drifted from the fire behind him.

The beast rose from its place and followed him silently, keeping just close enough to share the silence.

Derwin sat on a stone at the edge of the grove, staring out at the trees.

He closed his eyes.

Wouldn't be surprised if he sold us out.

He wanted to say it wasn't true. That he hadn't run. That he'd made the best choice he could. But the truth was messier than that.

He had fled.

He'd believed staying would only bring more death.

But now… he wasn't sure if that belief had been wisdom or cowardice.

The beast lowered itself beside him, pressing its weight gently into his side.

Derwin let out a shaky breath.

"They might be right," he whispered. "Not about the deal… but the rest."

The beast huffed — a low, gruff exhale that almost sounded like disagreement.

Derwin smiled, barely. "You're just as bad at lying as I am."

They sat in silence, the forest breathing gently around them. Behind him, the fire burned. Children laughed. Some would remember this night as joy. Others would always see him in shadow.

And maybe that was the truth, too.

He had come back, but he hadn't come back whole.

Not yet.

Morning arrived in gold and green.

Sunlight filtered through the leaves in warm patches, and for the first time in years, Derwin found himself smiling without realizing it.

The children had woken early — their laughter already dancing across the grove. A few were drawing glyphs in the dirt with sticks. Others played hide-and-seek among the tents. Derwin sat on a flat stone near the firepit, his side bandaged, his staff leaning against his knee, watching them with tired but gentle eyes.

The beast lay sprawled in a patch of sun beside him, head resting on its forelegs. It had allowed Maelin to tie a flower-woven cord around one of its antlers, which it now wore with complete indifference.

The boy from the night before approached cautiously, hands clasped behind his back.

"Have you thought of a name yet?" he asked.

Derwin scratched at his beard, squinting at the beast. "Well, I thought of 'Old Mossfur,' but someone snorted so hard I took it as a no."

The boy giggled.

"I think he needs a strong name," the boy said. "Something with teeth."

Derwin grinned. "Alright then. You keep thinking. I'll take suggestions over breakfast."

He turned slightly as Maelin brought him a handful of foraged berries and a slice of fire-baked bread wrapped in leaves. He thanked her softly and reached for the food — when a shadow fell over him.

Mother Kesa stood nearby, her posture quiet but firm.

Derwin felt the weight in her gaze before she spoke.

"Walk with me," she said.

No request. Just a soft command wrapped in the voice of someone who never raised it unless she needed to.

He stood slowly, nodding to Maelin and the others. The beast lifted its head but did not rise — it knew better.

Kesa led him beyond the tents, past the grove's edge, to a stone path mostly swallowed by grass and root. They walked in silence for a while, surrounded by the hush of morning trees.

Then she stopped.

"This land has not healed."

"I know," Derwin replied. "I can feel it."

"There is a wound deeper than the one you carry. One that festers still." She turned to him. "You left because you believed staying would only lead to ruin. You may have been right."

He tensed. "But I—"

"I am not judging you," she said. "That was done last night, by those who needed to. I have no interest in old pain." She stepped forward. "But I do need to know what you are now, Derwin."

He looked away.

"I don't know," he said. "Not yet."

She nodded, unsurprised. "Then here is your first chance to find out." She reached into the folds of her cloak and pulled out a small wooden charm — an old druidic marker used for tracking paths or marking safe routes. This one was cracked. "Three days ago," she said, "two younglings set out to harvest wild garlic near the river bend. They were meant to return that night. They haven't."

Derwin's stomach tightened.

"Joram led a search party yesterday. They found signs of movement. Broken branches. Drag marks." She looked him in the eye — not pleading, not commanding. Just present. "I can send Joram again. Or I can send you."

Derwin's hands curled slowly into fists. "I've only just returned," he said. "They don't even trust me."

"Do you trust yourself?" Kesa asked.

He said nothing.

She offered him the charm.

"You came back to see if you were still something," she said. "This is the shape of that answer. Protect them. Or accept that you are not the protector you thought you were."

Her hand remained outstretched.

Derwin stared at it.

The charm was light. Carved from pine. Marked with three crescent glyphs — safe return, shield, mercy.

He took it.

"I'll leave at once."

She nodded, stepping back. “Good. Then whatever you find, you will not find it alone.”

He glanced behind him — and there, standing silently at the edge of the trees, the beast waited.

Of course it did.

Chapter Three

The morning air was crisp and damp with river mist as Derwin rode eastward through the trees — the first time he'd ridden anything in years, and never something quite like this.

The beast moved like flowing stone beneath him — each step heavy but smooth, its great limbs navigating root and rock with ease. It didn't seem bothered by the weight of him or the leather pack strapped behind the saddleless ridge of its spine. Its antlers brushed past low-hanging branches, scattering dew across the path behind them.

Derwin kept one hand on its thick fur, the other wrapped loosely around the leather cord of the tracking charm, which swayed from his wrist.

The pack strapped to him was full — rations, herbs, ointments, and binding wraps, all prepared at dawn by Mother Kesa and a pair of the older children. Someone had even tucked a small cloth pouch of dried fruit and a folded note inside, though Derwin hadn't dared read it yet.

The forest ahead was quiet, but not dead. No birdsong, but no threat either.

Just waiting.

He closed his eyes briefly, inhaling through his nose.

Feel the charm. Feel the pull.

He'd used them before — many times. A lost druid, a scattered group of foragers, even once to track a wounded stag. When the bond was strong, the charm would almost hum in the hand, pulling gently toward the missing soul's path. It was part magic, part memory. But this one… nothing.

The cord was still. The wood cold.

Derwin furrowed his brow and focused harder, pressing his palm flat around the carved glyphs.

Still nothing.

The beast let out a low breath as if sensing his frustration.

"I'm trying," Derwin muttered. "Believe it or not."

The charm remained inert.

He looked out over the trail — old but visible. The younglings had followed it days ago. Faint boot prints. Broken grass. A few bent branches with fresh scarring. They had passed this way. That much he could tell.

But beyond that…

The forest refused him.

"You're still not listening," he whispered under his breath, not sure if he meant the woods… or himself.

The beast paused briefly to sniff the air, then pressed forward without waiting for direction.

Derwin let it lead. It seemed to know better, anyway.

He sat back in the saddleless seat of muscle and moss and tried again to tune into the land — to feel for echoes in the root, whispers in the bark. But the silence was complete.

Not rejection, he reminded himself. Just absence. Like a voice that hasn't decided whether it wants to speak again.

The beast turned down a narrow incline and picked up pace.

A fresh path. Someone — or something — had passed here recently.

Derwin straightened in his seat, gripping the charm tighter.

They were getting close.

By the time the sun slipped behind the trees, Derwin and the beast had covered hundreds of acres riding uneven terrain.

They'd crossed through old growth, glided along a deer trail half-hidden by fern and fog, and followed the signs: a snapped vine, a child's footprint pressed in soft soil, a streak of dried blood that hadn't yet browned. The path was there — fragile, vanishing with every gust of wind — but they were on it.

Still, they were losing light.

By the time Derwin found a narrow outcropping beneath a twisted willow — the roots arched just enough to shelter them — night had swallowed the trees entirely.

He slid from the beast's back with a groan and leaned against the trunk. His limbs ached. His side throbbed with every breath. But he didn't rest. Not yet.

The beast curled nearby, eyes still open, watching the dark with slow, deliberate blinks.

Derwin unstrapped his pack, set his staff across his lap, and began preparing a small fire — just a spark and a flicker, buried under a fold of stones. Enough to warm water. Enough to keep the dark at bay.

As he dug through his pack for the flint, his fingers brushed the folded parchment. The note. He stared at it for a long moment, then pulled it free.

It was old paper, clearly written by more than one hand. A mess of scribbles, misspellings, and tiny pressed flowers — but legible enough:

> Dear Derwin,
>
> We knew you'd go. Maelin said the moment you walked into the firelight, you looked like someone who hadn't finished what he was born to do. We hope this helps. And we hope you come back.
>
> P.S. The beast should have a name. We voted.
>
> His name is Bramble.
>
> Because he's prickly, quiet, and soft underneath — just like someone else we know.
>
> Love,
> The Younglings

Derwin's breath caught halfway through reading. By the end, he wasn't smiling, exactly — but something in his chest softened, uncoiled. He traced the name with his thumb.

"Bramble," he said aloud.

The beast lifted its head.

Derwin looked over. “Do you like it?”

Bramble blinked.

Then, with a slow groan of effort, the beast rolled to its feet and settled down again beside him — closer this time, resting its flank against Derwin’s side.

Derwin chuckled quietly and folded the note back into the pouch. “They knew I’d come,” he whispered to the fire, “even when I didn’t.”

Hours passed.

The fire burned low. The stars overhead were a thin smear of silver behind the branches. Wind rustled through the grove, stirring leaves like whispers.

Derwin sat with his staff across his lap, his eyes half-closed. He’d been trying to listen — not with his ears, but his soul. Still no charm response. Still no pull from the glyph.

But Bramble shifted beside him, standing now, ears perked forward.

Derwin watched the beast’s posture change.

Focused. Confident.

It stepped into the dark ahead, sniffed the air once, then moved deliberately, no longer hesitant.

The thought came slowly… then all at once.

He reached down, pressed a hand to the earth.

Don't look through your own eyes, he thought. Not now.

Look through his.

He exhaled slowly. Closed his eyes.

"Grant me the beast's gaze," he whispered. "Not as a master. As a mirror."

For a moment — silence.

Then… a flicker.

A single heartbeat's whisper — not in his ears, but in his blood:

"Accepted."

The glyph on his charm glowed faintly in the dark.

And for the first time since his return, the forest whispered back.

He opened his eyes.

Shapes sharpened. Edges in the dark moved into focus. Scent became memory. The world smelled of crushed fern, river mud, and something sharp — like sweat and iron.

The trail ahead shimmered like disturbed water.

The younglings had gone this way.

And something else had followed.

Derwin rose to his feet, staff in hand.

"Come on, Bramble."

The beast turned, ready.

They vanished into the dark — not as strangers anymore, but as hunter and hound, guide and guardian, druid and beast.

They moved swiftly through the dark.

Where once Derwin would have hesitated with each turn — second-guessing every broken branch, every faint trail — now he followed the path of living signs with newfound certainty.

The ground itself spoke: compressed earth where feet had fallen too heavily, snapped vines near the lower boughs — children's height. Scuffed bark. The torn edge of a wool sleeve clinging to a thorned bush.

The charm pulsed faintly at his side, but it was no longer his guide. It was only confirmation of what his eyes — no, Bramble's eyes — already told him.

The beast led without needing reins, nose low, movement confident. Every time Bramble paused, Derwin followed his lead, testing the air, touching the soil, asking the world around them to speak.

And for the first time in years, it did.

Hours passed in shadowed rhythm — step, breath, branch. The moon was a thin curve overhead, filtered by high clouds and taller trees. The deeper woods were quieter, less forgiving. The birds had gone silent.

Something had passed through here.

Something that didn't belong.

Derwin crouched near a deep rut carved into the mud — not footprints, but drag marks. Something heavy. Fresh.

He touched the rim. Still damp.

He stood slowly. “They're close.”

Bramble sniffed once, then turned toward the east.

A sharp scent hit Derwin a second later — metallic, foul. Blood. But not fresh. Old. Spoiled.

He moved faster now, Bramble taking the lead again. The underbrush thickened. The trees closed in. The wind stilled.

They came to a small ravine, carved by rain and time — and there, nestled awkwardly in the mud at the base, was a child’s satchel, half-buried.

Derwin slid down the incline, boots skidding. He reached for the satchel and turned it over.

Empty. Torn.

Inside, near the seam, a name stitched in soft thread: Lira.

His gut twisted.

He looked around.

The ravine ran into a narrow hollow — a place where water had once pooled but now stood dry. A cluster of trees leaned over it, unnaturally bent, as if pressed down by something heavy.

Derwin moved closer.

That's when the sound hit him.

Not a growl. Not speech.

A low, rhythmic wheezing — like something breathing that shouldn't still be alive.

Bramble stopped dead, ears raised, muscles tense.

Derwin dropped low behind a stone and peered over.

There, at the far edge of the hollow, hunched and twitching, was a shape he couldn't name.

It had once been a deer. Or something close. But its flesh was wrong — stretched too thin in some places, bloated in others. Its antlers were cracked and slick with sap-black blood, and its eyes glowed with a dull red film like heat behind dying coals.

Its breath rattled like wind through a broken flute.

Derwin felt the forest recoil slightly — a warning.

The corruption had touched this place.

And if the creature was a guardian of the grove, then something had twisted it into a sentinel of death.

He raised a hand slowly, whispering, "Not yet, Bramble."

The beast waited, still as stone.

Derwin gripped his staff and felt the whisper of magic rising just behind his skin — not eager, not loud, but ready.

The forest had answered him once.

Now it watched to see if he would answer back.

Derwin crouched behind the stone, fingers tightening around his staff as the wheezing of the corrupted beast echoed through the hollow.

It didn’t see them — not yet. But its breathing was irregular, twitchy, like something that had forgotten how to exist and was trying to relearn by force.

He swallowed hard.

The smell of rot clung to the air, filling and drying his mouth like ash. The trees whispered warnings again —
sharper now. Urgent.

Corruption. Blight. This one does not belong.

And then, like a fissure splitting open deep in his memory… he remembered.

Years ago – the day the forest cried

He’d been twelve.

It was late spring, and the sky above the grove had turned strange — overcast, not with clouds, but with something like smoke. The trees had trembled. Animals had fled long before he understood why.

Derwin had stood beneath the Heart Tree, clutching a leather satchel packed for a lesson he would never receive.

His mother had not come.

Neither had his father.

Instead, it had been Joram — younger, angrier, shouting at others to grab supplies. He had seen Derwin and looked away.

That was when the screaming started — not human, but the land.

The roots curled. The birds scattered. Something beneath the soil groaned in a way he didn't yet understand. It was grief, but too large for words. It moved through him like cold water down his spine.

He ran toward the edge of the grove.

That's where he saw them.

His parents. Rushing down the lower trail, packs full, cloaks tight, not looking back.

Not even at him.

He remembered calling out — calling out until he was sure they heard him.

Finally, his mother slowed.

She looked back.

There was no love in it. No guilt. Only a hard, grim acknowledgment — like she'd known he would be there, and had already decided to leave him behind.

Derwin took a step forward, and his father shouted something he would never forget. "You stay, boy. You want to be part of this forest so badly — then let it bury you with the rest."

And then they were gone.

That night, the roots twisted. A tree collapsed in the southern reach. The soil turned gray near the river. And the blight began.

No one ever said it out loud, but he knew.

They had done something.

And the forest — wounded by their betrayal — had never healed.

Derwin snapped back to the present with a sharp inhale, eyes wide.

The corrupted beast across the hollow twitched violently, its antlers gouging the soil as it sniffed the air. Its limbs didn't move like limbs — they crawled, dragging parts of itself that no longer worked.

His parents had fled from this.

And now, here it was — not as myth or symbol, but a living scar.

Derwin stood slowly, staff in hand.

The magic in his blood stirred — with purpose. The roots beneath his feet did not recoil. This time, they waited.

He reached for that memory — to hold it with clarity. "I'm not like you," he whispered. "You ran from this. I was born for it."

Beside him, Bramble growled low and steady.

Derwin stepped into the hollow, boots squelching in the muck.

The corrupted creature jerked its head toward him, red eyes flashing. Its limbs spasmed and flexed, cracking like sap-frozen bark. A low, bubbling hiss escaped its throat — the guttural sound of something half-dead trying to remember its own name.

Derwin raised his staff.

His body tensed with old instinct — but the motions were rusty. Loose. He had not fought in years, not like this, not with magic he no longer trusted to answer. But still he moved, settling into a half-remembered stance as Bramble growled beside him.

The corrupted guardian took a shuddering step forward.

Derwin whispered, "Let's see if the forest meant it."

The creature charged.

The first clash was pure chaos.

Derwin spun aside just in time to avoid the full force of the antlers, but a stray branchlike limb caught his side and sent him stumbling. He rolled through the mud, staff dragging behind him, heart slamming against his ribs.

Bramble launched past him in a blur of power and bone — crashing into the beasts' flank, knocking it off balance with a thundering impact that echoed through the ravine.

Derwin scrambled upright, channeling a burst of energy through his palm — the magic fizzled, sparked, then surged too late. Roots lashed out from the ground, but the beast had already moved.

It twisted with unnatural force and slammed its head into Bramble's side. The great beast let out a deep, rattling growl and staggered back.

Derwin gritted his teeth. "Focus."

He jabbed his staff into the soil, whispered a druidic phrase older than speech — and this time the land responded.

A ring of grasping vines shot up, wrapping around the creature's legs.

It shrieked — a sound too human, too broken.

Derwin moved to strike — but his footing slipped. The staff came down wide, missing its mark. The corrupted beast lunged again, snapping through the vines.

Cracked and rotten hooves raked across Derwin's shoulder. He cried out, dropping to one knee.

Before it could reach him again, Bramble slammed into the beast from the side, antlers crashing into corrupted bone. The two tumbled into the mud, locked together in a brutal tangle.

Derwin pulled himself upright, chest heaving.

He was losing.

But he was still fighting.

The beast and Bramble separated with a wet, heavy thud.

They circled.

Derwin lifted his staff, arm trembling, blood soaking into his robe.

And then—

A sound.

Faint.

To the left. Beyond the hollow.

A gasp.

A voice.

Small.

"Derwin?"

Everything stopped.

Bramble froze. The corrupted beast twitched, momentarily disoriented.

Derwin's head snapped toward the sound — eyes wide.

A child. Alive!

He stepped forward, uncertain if it had been real or memory — and then heard it again.

Closer.

"Help…"

Derwin looked toward Bramble, toward the enemy still writhing.

He gripped his staff tighter.

Chapter Four

Derwin's legs trembled beneath him. The taste of iron filled his mouth, and his breath came shallow and fast. Before him, the blighted beast — a once-sacred creature now twisted by corruption — staggered upright, steaming black ichor pouring from wounds.

His staff was cracked. His left hand barely responded. The weight of the moment pressed against his shoulders like the trees themselves were watching.

Behind him, Lira and Genn stared, frozen.

Derwin turned his head slightly, just enough to speak. "Bramble," he said, voice ragged, "take them. Now."

The great beast hesitated. A low, questioning growl.

"I'll hold it. Go."

"But Derwin—" Lira started, tears in her voice.

He didn't turn. "Please."

There was a moment of hesitation — then Bramble stepped forward, nudging the children gently but firmly with his snout.

Genn grabbed Lira's hand, and the two backed away slowly. Derwin heard their retreat — leaves rustling, Bramble's heavy hooves crunching the forest floor.

And then silence.

Just him.

And the beast.

It lunged.

Derwin raised his staff and met the charge. Roots burst from the ground, wrapping around limbs. His voice cracked as he called ancient words — not polished druidic, but raw need. The forest answered with a whisper.

The fight was brutal, sloppy. Derwin was too slow. The beast too fast. His shoulder took a glancing blow that sent him crashing to the ground. He rolled, barely avoiding the snapping jaws. His ribs screamed. He rose again.

Another spell. A blast of sunlight. The creature reeled.

Still it came.

A final clash — Derwin thrust the splintered staff upward, catching the beast beneath its ruined jaw. The corrupted body shuddered, limbs twitching — and with a rattling sigh, it collapsed.

He stood, trembling.

One step.

Two.

His knees buckled.

And the world vanished.

Branches above. Wind through trees. A child's breathless sobbing.

Derwin was running — small feet pounding earth, arms outstretched. "Mother! Father!"

Two shapes ahead, cloaked in bark-toned robes, moved fast through the woods.

They didn't turn back.

He tripped, caught himself, kept going.

"Please! Don't leave me!"

The shapes passed through a ring of standing stones — ancient and alive — and as Derwin reached for the gap, the forest shifted. Roots surged, bark groaned, and the path sealed behind them like a closing wound.

He stood alone in the clearing, breath ragged, heart hammering.

The wind picked up — not harsh, but mournful. The trees swayed with a language deeper than words. "They fled," the forest sighed, "left rot in their wake. Left you to carry it."

Derwin staggered to his knees, fists clenched. "Why me?" he asked, voice small. "Why didn't they take me with them?"

The forest replied, gentle but unyielding. "Because you were the only one they feared would remember."

Tears welled in his eyes. "I don't want this," he whispered.

"Want has never been the way of trees," the forest said. "But you are not them. You stayed." And as the whisper faded, he felt the weight of it all — abandonment, legacy, and the silent promise in the roots around him. “You are not the rot. You are the regrowth.”

Pain.

A dull throb through every limb. Cold air on his face. The world rocked gently.

Derwin cracked one eye open.

Above him, night trees swayed.

He was slumped across Bramble’s back, half-tied down with cloaks and rope.

“Don’t let go,” whispered Genn from somewhere beside him.

“I’m not,” Lira said, her voice firm despite its tremble. “He’s going to make it.”

Derwin tried to speak — a rasp, nothing more.

Warm light ahead. The smell of woodsmoke. The camp.

He slipped again into black.

The grove was quiet. Firelight flickered across elder faces. He was older now, but still small — hidden behind willow branches, breath held tight. The warmth of the fire didn't reach where he crouched, only the chill of what was being said.

Voices sharp and low:

"The blight began with them."

"He's their blood."

"He'll bring it back."

"He already has."

A pause. A long silence before another voice — gentler, uncertain. "He's just a boy. The forest hasn't rejected him. It speaks to him still."

"The forest is patient," snapped another elder. "Even rot can sleep beneath the bark."

"We should have cast him out when the others fled."

"And if we had?" came Kesa's voice, firmer now. "You would've turned your back on a child because of who bore him?"

A murmur of unease spread around the circle. Someone shifted on a log. The fire cracked.

"He shows signs," another elder said. "There's something wild in him."

"He communes with the trees," Kesa countered. "Better than most of you ever did."

"He's dangerous."
"So was the first druid who shaped life from nothing," she snapped. "Danger is not the same as corruption."

A heavy silence followed. Then one elder murmured, "We'll watch. But if there is even a sign – "

Kesa's voice cut through the firelight, quiet and cold. "You watched while his parents fled. You watched while he was left behind. And now you want to watch again? Cowards don't tend forests. They only wait for them to die."

The flames dimmed.

Derwin, small and unseen, clutched his knees to his chest. The words curled around him like vines. And yet, in the crackle of fading embers, he heard a whisper — the trees, gentle and honest. "Not theirs to name. Not theirs to bury. You are still growing."

He awoke to warmth and the scent of herbs. His ribs ached like splintered stone. A blanket — woolen and heavy — covered him. The flap of the healer's tent rustled gently in the morning breeze.

He tried to sit. A sharp spike of pain drove him back.

A firm hand pressed gently to his chest.

"Easy now," said Mother Kesa. She sat beside him, mixing salve in a stone bowl. Her face was drawn with exhaustion, but her hands remained steady. "You're lucky to be alive," she said. "And luckier still that Bramble listens better than you ever did."

Derwin gave a breath of a smile. "The kids?"

"Safe," she said. "Sleeping. Bramble hasn't left their side."

She turned and pointed.

Outside, just past the flap, Bramble lay curled like a guardian. Lira and Genn were asleep against his fur.

"They brought me back?" he murmured.

"They insisted," Kesa answered, her voice quiet. "They tied you down. Held on all night. You should've seen them yelling at the guards when we didn't let them into the tent."

Derwin's throat tightened.

"I had a dream," he said softly. "Not the kind that fades. One I lived before. I saw the fire, the elders. I heard what they said about me. About what I'd become."

Kesa's hands paused.

"They said I'd bring the blight back," he continued. "That I was dangerous. That I should've been cast out like my parents."

She didn't answer immediately. Instead, she placed the bowl down and folded her hands in her lap.

"They were afraid," she said. "But fear is a poor guide in sacred groves."

"You fought for me," he said, glancing at her.

"I did," she replied. "And I should have done more."

Derwin looked toward the tent flap. "I believed them," he said. "For a long time, I believed I was just rot waiting to bloom."

"You were a child," Kesa said, voice firm now, "a child who loved the trees and heard the wind. A child left behind by cowards."

He closed his eyes. "I hear the forest still," he whispered. "Even in that dream, when they spoke against me, the forest whispered different. It said I was still growing."

Kesa smiled faintly. "Then it sees you clearer than they ever did."

She reached forward and pressed a cool cloth to his forehead. "You stayed. You fought. And not for glory or redemption — for them. For the children. That's who you are."

A long silence passed.

"And that," she said gently, "is why you still belong here."

The flap rustled. Genn peeked in.

"Can I…?"

Kesa nodded. "Only for a moment." She stepped out.

Genn crept to the bedside, followed closely by Lira holding a folded piece of cloth. "We, um… we saved this," Lira said, holding out the note.

Derwin took it with shaking fingers.

"We knew you'd come back. We knew you'd fight. You just needed reminding who you are."

He let out a breath, touched the corner of his eye.

Genn glanced over at Bramble through the tent flap and grinned. “He hasn’t let anyone near us since we got back. Not even the grumpy guards.”

Lira stepped closer, her voice steady. “We don’t care what the rest of the camp says about you. We saw it.”

“Saw what?” Derwin asked, throat dry.

“You,” Lira answered, “stand between us and a monster. Bleeding. Scared. But not leaving.”

“You were stupid,” Genn added, trying not to smile.

“But brave,” Lira said firmly. “You could’ve run. You didn’t. That’s what matters to us.”

Derwin’s gaze dropped to the note again.

“You’re not who they say you are,” Genn said quietly. “You’re ours.”

Derwin blinked back the heat behind his eyes. “Thank you,” he whispered.

“Just… don’t leave again,” Lira said.

“Not unless you have to,” Genn added.

He nodded. “If I go, I promise… it’ll be to protect you.”

The children gave small smiles and turned to leave, brushing aside the tent flap. Bramble's eyes flicked open, watching them go.

As the children slipped out, the tent flap opened again. A figure stood silhouetted for a moment — tall, broad-shouldered, draped in worn forest robes. An older druid, his hair streaked with gray, eyes sharp as thorns. Marrec.

He stepped inside, arms crossed tightly. His gaze swept the tent, then fixed on Derwin. "So… you returned," he said, voice flat.

Derwin met his gaze but didn't speak.

"I wonder how long it'll be before we regret it," Marrec continued. "You know what they say — blight always comes back to its roots."

Mother Kesa stepped in from behind him, expression tight. "Marrec."

He didn't look at her. "We spent years keeping the rot at bay, and now we welcome its seed back into our heart?"

Derwin flinched.

"You weren't there," Kesa said, voice cold. "You didn't see what he did. You didn't see him stand alone."

"I saw what his parents left behind," Marrec growled. "Their shadow still lingers. Don't think the trees forget so easily."

Derwin finally spoke, his voice low. "I didn't come to be forgiven. I came to protect what I can. That's all I know how to do."

Marrec studied him for a moment, then gave a scoffing breath —

half laugh, half warning — and turned to leave. Before he stepped through the flap, he muttered, "Hope the forest is wiser than we were."

Kesa stood in silence for a moment, then turned back to Derwin.

"Some roots rot slowly," she said, softer now. "But even they can give rise to something new."

Derwin looked down at his hands, still trembling, still bandaged — but slowly, starting to steady.

Chapter Five

The forest had grown quieter during Derwin's recovery, but not still. The silence was a living thing — shifting, testing, never quite settling.

In the first days, he drifted in and out of consciousness on a cot in the healer's tent, pain spiking in waves through his ribs and shoulder. Each breath felt borrowed.

Yet the world beyond the canvas never let him drift too far.

Leaves whispered when there was no wind.

Roots flexed under his bedroll like restless muscles.

Birdsong came in brief flurries — sometimes bright and hurried, sometimes low and mournful.

And Bramble, ever watchful, paced in widening arcs outside, ears swiveling toward sounds only he seemed to hear.

The children came often. Genn would sit cross-legged by his cot, pretending to read for himself while quietly speaking the words aloud. Lira lingered near the tent entrance, fingers always busy — carving leather, weaving reeds, coaxing form from wood. Their presence steadied him more than he wanted to admit.

Kesa visited with herbs, salves, and teas, her voice a calm tether in the storm of his half-formed thoughts.

But the forest itself… the forest was the one pulling at him.

It wasn't calling for help. It was drawing him back — a wordless pull at the marrow, a quiet beckoning toward something that felt both inevitable and dangerous.

And every night, the same dream.

He was small again, legs aching as he ran through the woods, chasing the retreating figures of his parents. Their cloaks blurred into the trees, the distance between them always growing. The branches closed overhead, sealing like a wound.

The wind wept.

Firelight followed.

Faces in the dark. Elders' voices spitting judgment:

"He's their blood."

"He'll bring it back."

"We should have cast him out."

He always woke with those memories burning behind his eyes, the echo sharper than the pain in his ribs.

On the fifth morning, Kesa came without herbs. She sat beside him in silence for so long he almost thought she'd fallen asleep.

"I know what you've been dreaming," she said at last.

Derwin's gaze stayed on the tent wall.

"They were left for you," she continued, reaching into her cloak. "Your parents gave them to the grove in secret. I wasn't sure if you would ever want to see them."

She set a small bundle in his lap — violet-dyed linen, faded and fraying at the edges.

Inside lay a necklace woven from willow and copper wire, three charms shaped like phases of the moon hanging along its length. Beside it rested a narrow, curved dagger. Symbols, half-swallowed by time, wound along the hilt in a language he could almost — but not quite – understand.

When he touched the blade, it pulsed faintly, like the echo of a heartbeat.

He stared for a long moment. Neither object felt like a weapon against him — but neither felt safe.

They felt… desperate.

“Were they trying to protect me?” His voice was quieter than he meant it to be.

Kesa didn’t answer right away. “I think they were trying to protect something,” she said at last. “Perhaps from themselves.”

Derwin turned the dagger in his hands. The edge did not cut, though it was honed. The metal felt cold even in the warmth of the tent.

The moon-charms on the necklace chimed softly together, a sound too light for the weight in his chest.

From outside the tent, Bramble stirred. A low huff rolled

through the space, followed by the sound of heavy hooves shifting closer. The tent flap shifted, and the great beast’s head pushed through.

Bramble’s dark eyes fixed on the dagger. Not on Derwin. Not on Kesa. On the blade.

For a heartbeat, the beast stood motionless, ears slightly back, nostrils flaring. Then, with a quiet rumble, he withdrew and settled himself just outside again.

Derwin and Kesa exchanged a look neither tried to explain.

Kesa reached over and checked the binding around his ribs, her fingers gentle but firm. "That wound… should have been worse," she said finally. "The infection alone might have ended anyone else. If the blight had taken root—" She stopped herself, then shook her head.

"You're saying I'm lucky."

Her mouth curved faintly, though her eyes didn't soften. "Perhaps. The children brought you back quickly. The herbs I grow are strong. Maybe both." She hesitated just a moment too long. "Or… something else entirely."

She didn't elaborate.

Derwin let the weight of her words settle. He wasn't sure if the heaviness in his chest was from the bindings… or from the truth she hadn't spoken aloud.

He looked down at the dagger again, its etched symbols catching the light like they were holding it, not reflecting it.

And he couldn't shake the feeling that whatever kept him alive… was the same thing the forest now wanted him to face.

It was late morning, two days later, when Genn and Lira stepped into the tent together, their faces set with determination. Bramble followed them partway in, only to stop and sit heavily by the entrance — alert, expectant.

"You're going to leave again," Lira said before Derwin could greet them.

He blinked. "I haven't decided that."

"But you will," Genn said. "Bramble knows. He's on edge."

Derwin glanced at the great beast — whose ears perked as if in agreement.

"We're coming with you," Lira said flatly. "You can't go out there alone again. We've seen what you're walking into."

Derwin sat up straighter, exhaling slowly. "You're brave," he said, "and I'm proud of that. But you're not coming."

They both opened their mouths to protest, but Derwin raised a hand.

"Not just because it's dangerous," he said. "But because someone has to stay here and keep this place strong. Someone has to remind the people what we're fighting for. You two — you're not just clever, you're trusted. The younger ones look up to you. If I fail… they'll need someone who understands the stakes."

Lira crossed her arms but didn't argue. Genn scowled at the floor, frustrated.

"Look after the others," Derwin said gently. "And I promise… I'll come back."

There was silence.

Then Genn turned and stormed out. Lira lingered a heartbeat longer, her jaw tight, then followed.

"Bramble!" Genn called from outside. "Come on!"

The beast looked to Derwin. The druid nodded softly.

With a reluctant huff, Bramble turned and followed the children.

The next evening, they returned.

No speeches. No arguments.

Just the two of them, arms full of wrapped leather and bark and vinework.

“It’s not perfect,” Genn muttered.

“But it’ll keep you steady,” Lira added. “And Bramble actually *likes* it.”

They set the saddle down by his bed.

“You’ll probably leave soon,” Lira said. “We figured this time you shouldn’t walk.”

Derwin, overwhelmed, just nodded.

“Oh,” Genn said, reaching into a pouch. “And Mother

Kesa wanted you to have these.” Two slender vials dark green liquid swirling inside. “She said… and I quote,” Genn smirked, “if you insist on getting yourself hurt again, at least don’t make her walk out and drag you home.”

Derwin laughed, eyes damp.

He didn’t say goodbye. But he did say, “Thank you.”

That night, the whisper returned — but this time, it came with shape.

Derwin lay on his side, half-wrapped in his cloak, the necklace from his parents strung across his fingers. The charms felt heavier than they should have, as though they pulled his thoughts downward.

He blinked, once… and was no longer in the tent.

He soared above the treetops — but not by will. His spirit was dragged through the canopy like a leaf in a storm. Below, the forest churned. Blight spread in ribbons and veins, bleeding across the roots. Trees blackened. Branches curled. Animals fled in all directions. Some… not fast enough.

The sickness spread faster than he'd seen before. Something — someone — was pushing it, feeding it, forcing it deeper into the unspoiled wilds.

A shadow moved ahead of the blight like a herald. Cloaked, shrouded, faceless. Derwin felt both drawn to it… and sickened.

Was this a warning of what he was meant to stop? Or a vision of what he was fated to become?

He snapped awake, heart pounding.

The saddle sat quietly by the cot.

The dagger was cold in his hand.

And outside, Bramble let out a low, anxious groan.

The morning sun crept over the treetops, gold light brushing the edges of the camp. Derwin moved with care, wrapping the gifts and supplies left for him into his pack. He stepped slowly, still favoring his side, but there was purpose in every motion.

Before leaving, he sat beneath the broad-boughed gathering tree, a bowl of hot root stew in hand. Genn and Lira joined him on either side, eating quietly. Other children gathered nearby, pretending not to watch him too closely. Bramble lay stretched out in the shade, resting but alert.

Derwin smiled at the warmth around him. It didn't erase the tension in the air, but it softened it.

Mother Kesa arrived last, carrying a second bowl and sitting beside him with a quiet sigh. "This is the last quiet meal you'll have for a while," she said. "You should enjoy it."

Derwin nodded. "That's what I'm trying to do."

They sat in companionable silence a while longer before she spoke again.

"You've always been searching, Derwin. Even before all this. But sometimes the way forward isn't through the answer. It's through the asking. Don't lose that."

He looked to her, eyes heavy but grateful. "The forest showed me something last night," he said. "A vision. Stronger than any I've had before."

Kesa shifted, her attention sharpening. "Tell me."

Derwin set down the bowl, his voice quiet. "I was pulled through the trees, above the canopy, like I was caught in a current. Below me, the blight spread faster than I'd ever seen. It was alive… hungry. And someone's feeding it. Driving it." He hesitated. "I don't know if I was being warned… or tempted. But something wants me to follow."

Kesa was silent for a long time. Then she reached out and took his hand. "You're not cursed for the blood you carry, Derwin. You're blessed for the heart you haven't lost."

He blinked at her, surprised.

"Go," she said, "But go as *you.* Not as what the forest fears. Not as what the camp expects. Not even as what your parents were. Go as the boy who sat under the trees teaching the little ones how to breathe life into seeds."

Derwin swallowed hard and nodded.

When Bramble approached, saddle secure and stature calm, Derwin mounted carefully.

At the edge of the camp, he paused.

Genn and Lira were there, waiting. No words. Just nods.

Just trust.

Derwin nodded back.

And then, without looking back again, he rode into the forest.

CHAPTER SIX

The morning air was heavy with mist, clinging to the undergrowth in long fingers of dew. Derwin rode in silence, Bramble's steady gait the only rhythm to match the hum of the forest. What remained of the old path was swallowed by roots and rot, the trees more twisted now than they had been just days ago. The deeper they went, the more it felt like the forest was holding its breath.

Despite the weight of his mission and the quiet urgency that had taken root in his chest, Derwin couldn't help but glance at the children's saddle. It rested beneath him, hand-stitched and a little uneven, but strong. He could almost hear Genn's proud explanation, Lira's bashful smile.

"You'll come back," Lira had said. "But you'll ride right next to us next time."

He hoped she was right.

The forest around them whispered in strange ways. Birdsongs came in unfamiliar rhythms. Leaves twitched without wind. And always, somewhere deeper, the groan of something not quite dead.

They moved cautiously, weaving through bramble-thick trails and half-collapsed ruins long overtaken by moss and vine. The trees stood like ancient sentinels, their branches entangled above like judgmental elders watching in silence. Here and there, Derwin would pause — to feel the bark, to taste the air, to sense for the tremble beneath his boots that might lead them truer. But the forest gave only glimpses. A flutter of leaves without wind. A shimmer of light between trunks that vanished when pursued.

Twice they found animal tracks — not fleeing, but circling. Watching. Derwin began to suspect he was being followed, but Bramble remained calm. Whatever it was, it was not hunting.

They crossed a shallow stream that had turned murky with silt. Derwin touched the water and flinched. It wasn't poisoned — not yet — but it was fading, its energy drained by something nearby. The blight was close.

As dusk settled, shadows grew long and stretched like claws across the earth. A low mist began to roll in, curling around Bramble's legs. The quiet turned weighty. Still.

That's when they saw it.

Derwin dismounted and approached cautiously. The ruins were older than even the grove's founding stones. The air shifted here—thicker, charged with memory. A circle of shattered pillars framed the clearing, and at its center, the Eldest Heart Tree.

Or what remained of it.

Once a towering beacon of natural magic, it now stood hollow and blackened, its bark split with veins of gray. But Derwin still felt it — not gone, just… quiet.

He stepped forward, hand resting gently on Bramble's neck before moving away. At the tree's base, an old root bulged unnaturally. A subtle glint caught his eye.

He knelt.

There, nestled in a hollow knot of wood, was a sealed scroll and a vial of glowing liquid — soft white-gold like captured dawn.

The vision struck like a thunderclap.

Derwin staggered, falling to his knees as the world around him dimmed. A pulse echoed from the heartwood. Visions flickered before his eyes: his mother whispering incantations, his father burying the glowing vial beside the roots, both arguing with elders who pleaded for them to stop. A third figure stood apart — cloaked, face hidden, watching.

The figure did not speak, but Derwin could feel the tension — this was not a stranger. This was someone who wanted them to do what they were doing. Someone who had promised power in return for cooperation. The feeling clung like frost — a presence of unnatural hunger.

Then came the sight of a grove — not his, but a darker mirror. Twisted trees, red-lit torches, stone circles stained with old magic. A gathering of cloaked druids. And the figure among them — the same one. Their leader.

Derwin gasped, clutching his chest.

A voice spoke — echoing in his head.

"The seed does not choose the soil... but it may cleanse it."

He saw the blight's birth. Found. Prodded. Cultivated.
Then unleashed — not by rage, but by pride.

Then — a memory. Not vision, but something buried deeper.

Derwin was small, no older than five. The forest had been quieter then, still lush with summer bloom. He remembered the way the sun spilled through the leaves, the trail his mother and father had followed through the underbrush — not knowing he had crept after them.

They spoke in hushed tones. He couldn't hear the words, only their urgency. When his father pulled a leather-bound satchel from beneath his cloak, something in Derwin's chest twisted. He stepped forward, a stick cracking beneath his foot.

They turned. Fear — no, shame. His mother whispered something sharp. His father's expression fell.

"Go home, Derwin," his father said. But he didn't listen.

He followed them farther. Deeper. Until the forest changed.

The warmth faded. The trees lost their color. A smell like copper and rot filled the air. It hurt to breathe.

Then — the sound. A low, pulsing thrum, as if the earth itself was groaning.

Blight.

It seeped from cracks in the roots. Spread across bark like infection. Derwin's parents turned and ran — not toward him, but away. He screamed after them. Chased them.

He slipped.

Fell into a patch of the blight, arms outstretched.

It should have burned. Should have taken him.

But instead — silence.

Then light.

He woke in the grove, lying beneath the ancient tree, wrapped in vines like arms. Kesa sat nearby, her expression unreadable. No one asked what had happened. No one told him how he returned.

And he never saw his parents again.

The vision faded and Derwin's breath returned in sharp gulps. His parents' dagger suddenly trembled in his hand.

He looked up at the Heart Tree. Even now, split and hollowed, he could feel its will — quiet but insistent. It had wanted him to see. Not to punish, but to understand. It was not just a memory—it was a message.

He could feel it in the bark he rested against. In the heartbeat that echoed faintly through the roots. This tree had called him here.

"What am I meant to be?" he whispered.

Bramble nudged him gently. Derwin reached up and ran a hand through the creature's mane. The forest around them remained hushed. Waiting.

The scroll in his lap bore the crest of the First Circle. Its contents were cryptic, sealed with symbols he did not recognize — old druidic, perhaps. Derwin didn't know what the scroll contained or what it meant, only that it pulsed faintly with magic, waiting to be understood.

Derwin stared up at the hollowed tree. Even dead, it loomed with dignity.

"I don't know if I'm enough," he murmured.

But he packed the items carefully. He would carry them forward — just in case.

And for the first time in years, the wind rustled the leaves above.

The forest had heard him.

Chapter Seven

The trees grew quiet as Derwin and Bramble descended from the hollow ridge. The Heart Tree — now behind them — had left something within him stirring. Not just the memories or the scroll tucked deep in his pack, but a pulse of purpose. Fragile, maybe, but alive.

The wind whispered less now. Or perhaps it spoke more softly to test if he would still listen. He did.

They moved slowly. The deeper they went, the more the forest resembled a place between two worlds — not quite dead, not fully alive. Spores floated like ash. Roots bulged in strange patterns. Once-green leaves dulled to gray.

And yet… nothing attacked.

Creatures emerged from the brush, one by one. A fox with bleeding eyes. A boar whose skin pulsed with fungal threads. A great owl whose feathers were stiff with soot. None came closer. None ran. They stood watching — alert, twitching, waiting.

Derwin kept his eyes low, posture soft. He didn't call to the forest. He let it call to him.

At one point, he noticed the fox again — closer this time, no more than ten strides away. Its ribs rose and fell with uneven breaths, its eyes glassy and rimmed with blight. But it didn't growl or bare teeth. It only trembled, torn between the urge to flee and something else — a tethering, invisible and cruel.

Derwin took a cautious step forward. "You don't want this," he whispered. "Do you?"

The fox flinched, its body locking tight. Derwin stopped, crouching slightly.

"I can feel it. You're not gone. Not completely."

He reached slowly into his pouch and pulled out a sprig of crushed thyme, letting the scent drift on the air. The fox's nose twitched. Its eyes fluttered — confusion, pain, maybe recognition. Then, in a single swift motion, it turned and darted into the underbrush.

Derwin stayed crouched long after it vanished.

"They don't want this," he murmured. "They're stuck... and something is holding them there."

When they finally stopped to rest, he knelt beside a slow stream trickling beneath a tangle of roots. He washed his face, then peeled away the bandages across his ribs and shoulder. The wound he'd taken during the fight to protect the children had begun to close. No rot. No sickness.

His hands trembled.

He recalled the grove healers whispering how even touching a blighted beast could doom you. And yet he had bled from it. Bathed in its blood. And now, he was healing.

"I should be sick," he whispered.

Bramble let out a low rumble and nudged Derwin's shoulder.

"I'm not," Derwin said. "I'm not like them."

He thought of the child he had been. Of the vines that wrapped him gently all those years ago. Of waking up in the grove when he should've been dead. The elders never told him how he came back. Maybe now, he understood.

He was immune.

But why?

As the sun bled into the horizon, Derwin repacked his herbs and cloth, then stood. Around them, the infected creatures remained just out of reach — their stares never wavered.

That night, storm clouds rolled across the sky like slow, seething spirits. Derwin found shelter in the rocky mouth of a shallow cave. Bramble nudged inside behind, curling tightly and exhaling long and low. Derwin started a small fire with what dry kindling he could gather and settled into his cloak.

But they weren't alone.

The rustling outside wasn't wind. A low snort echoed in the trees. Derwin stood, tense, his hand near his staff. Bramble rose too, alert but unafraid.

Then, through the rain, three hulking shapes emerged — a family of bears, fur matted, eyes wary but not blighted. A mother and two older cubs, seeking shelter.

Derwin froze, unsure.

The mother bear gave a soft grunt, almost like a request. Bramble didn't growl. Didn't move. He looked at

Derwin, waiting.

Derwin slowly stepped aside, gesturing to the far end of the cave. "It's big enough," he whispered.

The bears entered, careful but calm. They lay opposite Derwin and Bramble, water dripping from their coats. For long minutes, nothing but the fire's crackle filled the silence.

Eventually, one of the cubs let out a soft huff and rested its head on its paws. The mother's breathing slowed. Derwin watched them, eyes wide — not in fear, but awe.

"This forest still remembers," he whispered. "Even in all this..." He leaned back against Bramble, who rumbled contentedly behind him. "I don't know what I'm becoming," Derwin murmured, "but I think... I think it's something I was always meant to be."

Outside, the storm wept. Inside, surrounded by beasts that should've torn each other apart, there was only warmth.

Derwin drifted to sleep with firelight on his face and peace — strange and rare — in his chest.

At first light, Derwin stirred. The bears were gone — quiet as they had come. The coals had long since died, but Bramble stood at the cave's mouth, muscles tense.

"What is it?" Derwin asked, rising and brushing sleep from his eyes.

Bramble didn't turn, only stared ahead.

Derwin stepped beside him and followed his gaze.

There, not far from the clearing, stood a tree with blackened bark. Embedded in its trunk was a strange totem — carved from bone and wood, pulsing faintly with corrupted magic. It thrummed like a heartbeat, but off-rhythm, diseased.

Derwin approached, hand outstretched. The closer he got, the more wrong the air felt — heavy, charged, whispering things in no tongue he knew.

He touched it.

A flash.

A feeling — dread, old and vast. The weight of eyes watching. The sense of a path diverging ahead, one step from safety.

He pulled back, breath ragged.

"This... this was left to mark something," he whispered. "Or call something forward." He turned to Bramble, now at his side. "We follow it, like we followed the charm. But this one..." He looked back once more at the totem, then mounted Bramble with a grim breath. "This one feels like it doesn't want to be followed."

They pressed on — into something darker. The watchers had parted.

Now the forest waited.

Chapter Eight

The totem's pulse became their compass.

It throbbed in the bark behind them like a second heartbeat, and Derwin followed its echo through soil and root the way he'd followed the search charm. This was darker—its pull like cold iron—yet familiar enough to trace. He let his palm trail the trunks as they went, listening for the subtle tremor that answered from deep below.

The forest changed in increments. First, the moss lost its spring and clung like damp cloth. Then the ferns thinned into brittle fronds that crackled at a touch. Vines hung in curtains from the canopy, weighted with black pods that clicked open and shut, tasting the air. Pools appeared between the roots—glass-still, with a sheen that reflected the sky the wrong color.

Bramble halted twice, shoulders hard as stone. The first time, he simply stared downwind until the breeze shifted. The second, he pawed a circle into the loam and grumbled low, a warning as much as a question.

"I feel it too," Derwin murmured, laying a hand against the great beast's neck. "We keep to the edges."

Signs of habitation emerged by degrees. A rack of drying herbs lacquered with tar-black resin. A lattice of thorn-canes woven into cages no larger than a man's torso—empty now, but fur still clung to the thorns. Footprints that began clean and booted and ended smeared, as if the ground had tried to swallow them.

By late morning the hum underfoot had gathered into a nervous, constant shiver. The trees opened to a low bowl of land ringed in black-thorn. Sap wept from the thorns and climbed the bark instead of falling, rejoining the branch like a reversed tear. In the bowl's center, stones rose in a warped circle—once a grove site, but no longer sacred. The air above it bent light in tight ripples, as if the heat of summer pressed down though the day was cool.

Derwin slid from Bramble and sank into a crouch behind a blown-over trunk. He listened.

Not chanting. Not exactly. A susurrus of breath shaped into pattern—like someone teaching children to hum a melody until it became a single note. The smell of crushed bitterleaf and old blood lay like a film over the clearing.

He crept the perimeter, moving slow, staff low. From this angle, he saw them: five cloaked figures tended the circle. Two knelt at the stones, pressing blighted vines into carved grooves that zigzagged like lightning across their faces. Another sprinkled powder that smoked where it fell. The last two stood watch, staves banded with iron. Their hoods were up, faces masked in bark-shells etched with spirals that made Derwin's eyes ache if he stared too long.

A shape twitched near the altar.

A fawn—alive, bound with thorn-canes, eyes wide and rimmed in gray. One of the kneeling figures hovered a hand over its chest. The fawn's breathing hitched in unnatural rhythm, as if the air itself refused to choose whether to give or take.

Derwin's jaw set. He reached for the forest—careful, cautious. He did not call for power; he asked for permission. A tremor answered from the roots, wary but listening.

Across the clearing, a watcher turned. The mask tilted, as if scenting. Their staff ticked once against the stone.

Derwin stilled.

A voice rose from within the circle—not loud, but precise. “Bind. Hold. Inward.” The hum tightened. The vines along the stones twitched as if breathing.

He could not wait. He lifted two fingers and traced a small glyph in the loam for quiet passage, then signed low to Bramble: circle, flank, stay unseen. Bramble melted into shadow with a softness that belied his size.

Derwin slid closer to the fawn’s side of the ring. Heat rolled off the stones in waves. The grooves in them weren’t druidic sigils; they were their reflections, warped—growth rewritten into recursion, seed into hunger. He felt it in his teeth.

“Easy,” he breathed to the fawn. Its gaze skittered to him. He pressed his palm to the soil outside the circle and whispered the smallest of boons, the one he taught first to children: borrowed breath.

A cool thread of air passed beneath the thorn-canes and into the fawn’s lungs. Its panic eased by a hair.

The watcher closest to Derwin tensed.

“Show yourself,” they said, voice muffled by bark.

Derwin rose slowly, hands open, staff across his back. “I’m not here to harm you.”

“That is a pity,” the watcher replied, stepping closer. “Harm is a teacher the Circle abandoned.”

“Who are you?” Derwin asked.

"Caretakers," they said. "Of what your elders were too timid to understand."

Derwin's gaze flicked to the fawn, then the stones. "You're breaking it. The land. The rites. Children."

"Children?" the watcher's head tilted. "We do not take. We offer. Some are brave enough to accept what the forest truly is."

Across the ring, a second masked figure called without looking up, "The Apprentice speaks well of the teacher who fled. Says he taught her to listen."

A cold knot formed beneath Derwin's sternum. He kept his voice level. "Where is she?"

"Farther than you can follow," the watcher said. "Closer than you deserve."

The ground within the stone ring split with a wet crack. A limb like a root—but jointed—levered itself up from the soil, followed by a hunched torso plated in bark-scales that oozed sap. Hollow sockets glowed with a sickly green sheen. It had a druid's silhouette, once. Now it was a mockery.

"Let it test you," the watcher said. "Let the forest decide."

They and the others stepped back into the brambles, bodies dissolving into shadow as if the thorns themselves had swallowed them.

Derwin exhaled once and moved.

The thing lunged with clattering speed. Derwin rolled, snapped his staff across the creature's knee-joint, and felt the wood jar against something half-stone. He thrust his palm to the earth.

Vines answered him—late, thin, but present—snaking up to grip the monster's ankles. The hold faltered almost as soon as it found purchase, as if the ground itself were second-guessing the command.

"Stay with me," he hissed to the roots. "Not as master. As mender."

The vines held for a breath longer. It was enough. Bramble crashed from the brush like a falling tree and hammered the creature with an antlered sweep. Bark-scales splintered. Sap sprayed.

The guardian reeled, then vomited a jet of black resin that hissed where it struck the soil. Spatters kissed Derwin's bracer and smoked without biting—a wrongness that recognized him and slid off anyway. Derwin felt the shock of it and bit down on the question. Later.

He lifted his staff and traced a purifying arc. Light gathered—thin, stubborn—along the tip, then faltered as if smothered by a wet cloth. He forced the motion through, driving the glow into the guardian's chest. It shrieked; the light sputtered to embers.

Bramble took the opening, ramming the monster back into the stones. One of the warped grooves cracked.

The clearing reacted.

Roots convulsed, rising like snakes to lash Derwin's calves. He leapt, stumbled, caught himself on one knee. The canopy sagged, leaves clumping to choke the light. Every call he made to the earth came slower, like speaking underwater.

"Alright," he breathed, setting his stance. "Defense, then."

He shifted to interception—staff catching joint and jaw, palm flicking small bursts of cleansing through each contact, not enough to burn the rot out but enough to sting it back. Bramble harried the flanks, refusing the thing a clean charge. Twice the guardian feinted past Derwin to spit resin at Bramble; twice Derwin slid in to take the blow, the stuff sliding from his skin with a greasy shiver that left him shaken and unharmed.

From the brambles, whispers. "He bends it." "It does not take." "The bloodline."

He ignored them. He could not afford anger.

The fawn coughed—a weak, human little sound that cut like a blade. Derwin pivoted toward it and slammed his staff point-first into the soil, throwing everything he had into a circle no wider than the bound creature. The ground under the fawn cooled. The thorn-canes loosened by the width of a fingernail. Its eyes cleared for a heartbeat and found him.

"Breathe," he whispered.

The guardian seized the moment and slammed into his exposed side. Derwin flew, struck a stone, saw stars. Pain sang along his ribs; old wounds protested. He tasted blood.

Bramble roared—no word in it, only fury—and drove the monster away from Derwin's crumpled body, hooves churning the loam. Antlers locked with root-limbs in a grinding contest.

Derwin clawed to his knees and pressed a palm flat to the earth. He did not ask for power. He offered a bargain.

"Not to kill," he whispered to the ground. "To end suffering. Yours, mine, theirs."

Something yielded—a memory beneath it. Cool water. Spring sunlight. A child's palm on warm stone.

A thin vein of clean magic threaded his fingers.

He surged to his feet, drove that line along his staff, and swept a narrow, exacting cut across the guardian's chest—not a blow to break, but a suture to close. The light stitched where it passed. The creature spasmed, then stilled—not healed, not whole, but quieted, the rage bled out of it.

It slumped against the stones with a sound like wet bark giving way. Sap leaked clear for a breath, then darkened again.

Derwin stood panting, staff tip smoking. Bramble backed away, sides heaving, head low.

A slow clap sounded from the thorns.

The masked watcher emerged only halfway this time. "Timid. Wasteful. But… instructive."

Derwin lifted his staff. "Release the fawn."

"It will be released when it serves its lesson," the watcher said. "As will you." Their mask cocked to the side. "Tell your camp the Apprentice thrives. Tell them she asked about you."

Rage flared—hot, clean. Derwin stepped forward—and the watcher blurred. Bark and cloth unraveled into shadow and were gone. The other figures had vanished with them, as if they had never been.

The hum under the soil eased. The warped circle did not.

Derwin stumbled to the fawn and cut the thorns with his knife, careful as a surgeon. “Easy,” he breathed. “Easy.” The last loop fell away. The creature shivered, staggered to unsteady legs, and bolted for the brush, pausing only once to look back with eyes a shade less clouded than before.

Derwin watched it vanish, chest aching in ways bone and sinew could not explain.

He wiped sap from his hands that would not stain. He could feel the grove like a wound under a scar—quiet for the moment, not mended.

Bramble pressed his head to Derwin’s shoulder. The druid leaned into it, eyes closed.

“We’re not ready for them,” he whispered. “Not yet.” He glanced at the cracked groove in the stone. “But we’re not nothing, either.”

He scanned the clearing one last time. No sign of the masked figures. Only the warped circle, the racks, the cages, the echo of a hum he could not unhear.

He mounted Bramble with care and turned them back toward the trees’ edge, not retreating so much as resetting the line.

“We find Kesa,” he said. “We tell her what we saw. And we learn what this scroll wants from me.”

Behind them, the clearing seemed to inhale.

Ahead, the forest—wounded, waiting—made room for their passing.

CHAPTER NINE

The grove's shadows clung to Derwin long after he and Bramble left it behind. The air seemed heavier now, as though the trees themselves leaned closer, whispering things they didn't want him to hear.

The blight was thicker here — not in sight, but in feeling. It pressed against the skin, an oily wrongness that prickled the back of his neck. Bramble's ears twitched at every sound, muscles taut under his dark fur.

They followed no path. The forest offered none. Only the barest hint of direction tugged at Derwin's senses — a thread, faint and cold, guiding him through roots and brambles that snagged at his cloak.

By the time they reached the base of a gnarled willow, the forest had gone utterly still. Not a birdcall, not a stirring breeze. The air was so quiet—Derwin heard his own heartbeat.

Then, a voice.

It came from nowhere. Everywhere.

"Derwin of the Grove."

He froze. The sound was deep, patient, almost warm — but it slid into his thoughts like a thorn.

"You walk far from your home," the voice continued. "And yet, you walk closer to it than you've been in years."

Bramble bared his teeth at nothing.

Derwin tightened his grip on his staff. "Show yourself."

The mist between the willow's roots thickened, coiling upward into a silhouette. Not smoke. Not shadow. Something in between, shifting and stretching until the figure of a hooded druid stood before him. The face beneath was half-hidden, lit only by eyes the color of dying embers.

"I've no reason to harm you," the figure said. "In fact, I'm here to offer you a choice."

Derwin's jaw tightened. "You're behind this corruption."

The figure tilted his head. "Not behind it. With it. Shaping it, guiding it. As your parents once tried to do."

The words hit like a thrown stone. "You don't know anything about my parents."

"I know they were not the first to see potential in the blight," the druid said, voice calm, unhurried, "and I know they understood something your grove never did — that to change the forest, you must first break it."

Derwin's breath came sharp through his teeth. "You've convinced others of this madness?"

A slow smile crept across the druid's mouth. "Some of your younglings already stand with me. They speak of you fondly. You taught them well… though I teach them better."

The words were bait — and they found their mark.

"No one from my grove would join you willingly," Derwin snapped, stepping forward.

The druid's ember eyes glimmered. "Willingly? No. But once they see the truth, they stay."

Derwin swung his staff, the strike passing through the figure like a shadow. The druid's form wavered, then split into a dozen silhouettes before melting back into the mist.

"Not here," the voice whispered around him now. "Not yet. But soon, Derwin. When you've seen enough… you will understand that my path is the only path left."

The mist thinned. The voice faded.

Derwin stood trembling — from the sharp, seething certainty that none of this was over.

Bramble stepped close, pressing his head to Derwin's shoulder.

"I know," he murmured. "Let's move."

But the words the druid had left him with clung to his mind like burrs.

Bramble kept pace beside him as they moved on, but the forest felt different now — heavier, like the ground itself was holding its breath. The wind hissed through the leaves in uneven sighs, each one carrying the faint echo of that voice.

Some of your younglings already stand with me...

Derwin clenched his jaw, forcing his thoughts forward. The words were meant to dig under his skin, to make him doubt, to slow him down. But what if—

He stopped walking.

Bramble halted too, looking back at him.

"What if it's true?" he muttered aloud. "What if someone did follow him? If he found one of them lost, alone, and told them his lies before we could reach them…"

The idea tasted like rot in his mouth.

Memories surfaced without permission — the days teaching the younglings to track animal prints in mud, to weave poultices from forest herbs, to listen to the song of the wind and hear meaning. He'd seen the way they looked at him, eyes bright with trust.

And now the image twisted. Those same eyes clouded with blight, staring at him from the other side.

His fingers tightened on his staff until the wood creaked. "Not a single one went willingly," he whispered. "Not one."

Bramble pressed his flank against Derwin's side, a silent weight grounding him.

The path ahead curved into shadow, roots rising like ribs from the earth. Derwin forced his steps forward.

"Come on," he said again, voice steadier. "If they're out there, we'll find them before he does."

The wind stirred. No voice answered this time. Only the faint rustle of leaves — as though the forest itself approved, but knew the road ahead would cost him more than he yet understood.

Chapter Ten

The blight's grip on the land was tighter here, clinging to every branch and shadow. All day Derwin and Bramble had forced their way through snarled thickets and poisoned streams, where minnows floated belly-up and reeds wore a soot-dark sheen. It had been far easier to enter this corrupted stretch than to find their way out. Without the charm to guide them, every turn felt like walking deeper into a maze that wanted them lost.

They marked their passing with small mercies—Derwin cutting a choking vine free from a birch, whispering a cooling breath over a fevered patch of moss, Bramble shouldering aside deadfall without crushing the ferns beneath—but the forest's mood did not lift. Even the wind sounded wrong, like breath drawn through cracked glass.

By nightfall, they found a narrow clearing beneath a leaning pine. Bramble lay close, a living wall between Derwin and the black-stained dark beyond. The fire sputtered weakly; every spark seemed to flinch. Cold carried whispers. Sleep came reluctantly—the way a stunned animal collapses more than rests—and with it, the vision.

He was not himself. Not entirely. The world tilted and he was looking from a different height, with a steadier gaze, through eyes that had learned to measure before leaping.

He was looking through Ashling's eyes.

Before

The grove as she remembered it was made of small details. The way light gathered on the teaching circle's stones, warm even in winter. The creak of the Heart Tree's high limbs when the weather turned. The smell of fresh bread the little ones brought, still wrapped in their mothers' scarves, because lessons always ran long.

And him—

Derwin, barefoot on the moss, showing how patient hands and quiet breath did more than force ever could. He said things that sounded like jokes until they weren't: "Don't ask the seed to wake up. Sit beside it until it feels safe knowing you're there." He tapped her brow once and said, "Balance." He said he would keep them safe the way roots keep a hillside from sliding; you didn't see it most days, but you felt it when it mattered.

He showed her how to tell when the ground had slept badly. How to thank a fallen branch before carving it into a whistle. How to bow to a river without kneeling.

She kept the first sprout she ever coaxed alive in a chipped clay cup, moving it around the communal hall to follow patches of sun. When it outgrew the cup she planted it by the south path and visited it every morning, just to touch the leaves and report what the wind had said at dawn.

Sometimes Derwin walked her back from the lesson stones. He didn't speak; he didn't need to. But when he did, he told stories about birds who taught themselves to swim and stones who learned to float for a single day of the year. She never knew which ones were true and which ones were spells to make her look up.

The day she bound her name-mark on the handprint tree—hers a little crooked, sap smearing her knuckles—Derwin tied a violet thread around her wrist and said, "You listen with more than your ears. That's rare. We'll make a druid of you yet, Ash."

Ash. He was the only one who called her that without making it sound small.

On the night of the midyear fire, when the elders spoke about the first circles and the first Heart Trees, Derwin caught her sneaking a second honey cake and pretended not to see. Later she found half of his in her pocket. She told no one.

He had promised once—quietly, so it would not turn to smoke by being said too loud—that he would keep them safe. He said it like a truth he wanted to believe more than she did. She believed for the both of them.

The Day the Wind Changed

It wasn't a roar at first. It was the wrong kind of quiet. Birds stopped mid-note. The mushrooms under the north pines turned their caps down. The dogs at the edge of camp refused their food.

When the screaming started, it wasn't human. It was the land.

Ashling's cup plant trembled though no wind reached the hall. She grabbed her satchel without knowing why and ran.

Derwin was already outside, jaw tight, eyes on the western ridge. Joram shouted something about the southern trail. Mother Kesa's voice cut clean across the noise, "Gather the younglings. To the inner circle. Now."

Ashling ran toward Derwin because that was the shape of all her instincts. He looked at her—and the look said three things at once: Good, you came. Do what I said last lesson. I am afraid.

They moved. The ground felt too thin, like a drumhead stretched to tearing. From somewhere beyond the cliffs, a breath like wet ash pushed through the trees and everything flinched.

Derwin herded them—kindness turned to command, voice low so panic would not hear it and grow. He put little Lina on his shoulders because she couldn't keep up. He handed Ashling the pouch of seeds because she remembered which ones liked to wake fast when soot was near. He said nothing about fear. He didn't have to; it was there in the set of his mouth.

They reached the inner circle and it looked wrong. The Heart Tree trembled in a way old wood should not. The elders argued in the language of people who have waited too long to argue.

Marrec said, "It has to be cut out." Someone else said, "We don't cut out the heart to cure a fever." Kesa said, "We move the children and then we speak."

Ashling held the pouch so tight the seeds imprinted on her palm. She searched the crowd for Derwin the way roots search for water. Found him at the edge, between two truths—one where he stood, one where he fled.

Joram pointed. Derwin looked. Ashling followed the line of their eyes and saw, just for a heartbeat, two cloaked figures on the lower trail, moving fast. One turned back. The angle of the mouth was familiar. Ashling did not understand until later.

Derwin took one step toward the lower trail—then three steps back, into shadow.

The wind changed. The smell of the blight slid beneath everything.

Ashling wanted to be braver than she was. She was thirteen. Bravery felt like a word adults said and hoped would choose them when it mattered.

Derwin came back— long enough to put the pouch in her hands. "You're fast," he said, like a benediction. "If something happens, you lead them east to the stream. Use the crescent markers. Don't wait for me."

"But you—"

"I will find you," he said. He made it sound like the end of an old story. He made it sound like a promise the forest would punish him for breaking.

She believed him.

After

Smoke and orders and the dull thud of axes cutting rope—dismantling the communal hall so it would not burn and take the ferns with it. The Heart Tree moaned once, and old bark split like skin in winter. The ground
went slick underfoot where sap pooled.

Ashling did as she was told. She led. She hauled. She counted heads and counted again and learned who to stop counting. She kept the little ones near, even the ones who thought they were too old to be called little. She used the crescent markers and found the stream. She slept not at all.

Derwin did not come.

On the second dawn, she went back to the grove edge with Maelin (who was still small then, all elbows and certainty) and left a braid of grass where Derwin had told stories. "So he knows

we're here," Maelin whispered. Ashling said nothing because words felt like lies if they were too hopeful.
On the fourth day, Joram returned with his sleeve torn and his mouth a straight cut. He said nothing useful. He did not say Derwin's name. The shape of that silence was a map to places Ashling could not let herself go.

On the seventh day, Mother Kesa found Ashling awake before dawn, fingers stained with coal from drawing crescent signs too close together. "You have to sleep," Kesa said. "We need you in the mornings."

"Derwin told me to lead them," she answered, daring Kesa to say what everyone else had decided.

Kesa did not. She only cupped Ashling's cheek and said, "You hear the forest the way he does. That is heavy and it is holy. It will make people afraid. Do the work anyway."

Ashling slept for an hour because Kesa asked it. In the dream she walked down the lower trail and caught a shadow by the wrist. It turned and it was Derwin and his face said I'm sorry and I was trying to save you by leaving you and I don't know how to carry the weight you put on me when you believed in me. When she woke, she punched a tree until bark scraped her knuckles and then wrapped the hand herself because she did not want Kesa to see her shaking.

Weeks made a camp out of grief. They moved east and then north; they learned where the blight caught slow and where it ran; they learned what to burn and what to bury. Ashling became the one who could find water when the ground lied about where it hid. She stopped wearing the violet thread because it got caught on things and because when people saw it they looked at her with a kind of pity that made her throat hurt.

She stopped leaving braids for Derwin. Then she started again, angrier. Then she stopped.

Whispers

The first time the whisper came, it was not from the trees. It slid along the edge of the fire's light and said, *You were promised a safety he could not give.* Ashling did not answer. The second time, it said, *You deserve a teacher who does not run.* She threw the voice a look sharp enough to cut bark. The third time, it said nothing at all, only stood at the treeline, more absence than shape, until Ashling stared back long enough to admit that where grief had been was now something harder.

She told no one. She trained. She learned to move when the ground warned her three breaths before danger. She stopped waiting for apologies that would not come. She learned magic at the edges of things—small, precise, good. A bruise pulled out of a child's shoulder and set into the bark of a maple to fade. A fever coaxed to leave by promising it a warm stone to sleep in until morning.

She wrote a letter she never sent:

> You promised to keep me safe and then you asked me to do the keeping. I did. I am still doing it. I don't know if I forgive you. I don't know if that matters.

The Chase

The vision dragged Derwin through these days as if his feet were tied to Ashling's shadow. When it shifted again, she was older. Her stride was an answer to a question no one had asked her permission to pose. She ran because it was the one thing that still felt like choosing.

Trees blurred. Roots rose. Wind tore past. She heard his voice behind her and felt two things at once: the old urge to turn and the newer, colder instinct to make him work for the right to be heard.

When his fingers finally closed around her wrist, she turned. He saw—through her eyes—the angle of his face when he was afraid and trying not to be. He saw the exact cut of the hurt she wore so he would not mistake it for simple anger. He saw the scowl and understood, in a way he had not allowed himself to, that it was not for that one day only. It was for every day she kept the promise he put in her hands when he fled.

"Let go," she said in the voice of someone who had learned how to walk away without asking permission.

He did. Because Ashling's eyes had no room left for old stories.

The Leaving

The world lurched—another shift. Smoke. Orders. The sound of axes. Derwin at the edge, a line drawn through him that ran from fear to duty to a place she could not follow. She saw him look back and she understood more than she had wanted to that he believed leaving would save them. That he could not make the thoughts align another way. That he was wrong, and also that he was hers.

He turned. He ran. And the part of her that loved him did not die. It did not forgive. It planted itself deep and learned to live with less light.

Derwin came back to himself like a man breaking ice to reach air. The clearing snapped into place around him—the lean of the pine, the hiss of the low fire. Bramble was standing now, head high, nostrils flared. Derwin's hand had already found the beast's mane and was clenched there hard enough to ache.

"Ashling," he said, the name a raw thing. He tasted smoke that wasn't there and heard the echo of a promise he had made too easily and broken too soon.

Bramble bumped him once, hard enough to be felt, gentle enough to be forgiven. The beast's eyes held steady, unjudging. Derwin rested his brow against the rough warmth and forced his breath to even out.

"I thought leaving would save you," he said into the night, and the confession made the dark shift, as if listening. "I thought I could be the villain for a day and spare you a lifetime of it. I was wrong."

He let himself sit in the wrongness without turning it into a weapon against himself. He let the hurt do what hurt does when it is finally named: become information.

The fire had collapsed to a red seam. He fed it two thin sticks and watched the flame decide whether to live. It did. He drank water that tasted of iron and old leaves and did not mind.

When he lay back down, sleep did not come. That was alright. He did not want to dream more of borrowed memories. He wanted to be awake enough to make a different one when the chance came.

At some hour with no name, he rose and walked the clearing's edge. In three places he found the blight's fine, black filaments threading between roots like hair in a comb. He did not burn them. He pressed his palm to the ground over each and said, quietly, "I left. I am here now. Make of both truths a path." The threads withdrew—not far, not conquered, but listening. Bramble followed his circle as if patrolling a boundary that had just been redrawn.

Dawn came thin and gray. Somewhere a thrush tried a fragile phrase and let it fall. Derwin saddled in silence, every motion deliberate. Before they left, he crouched and pressed two fingers to the earth where his bedroll had been.

"Ash," he said softly, using the name he hadn't said in years, "I hear you. I'm coming the right way this time—even if it's the long way."

Bramble knelt to make the mount easier. Derwin swung up and felt the ache in his ribs the way one feels the ache of a lesson finally learned.

They pushed north.

The forest did not grant a miracle for the apology he had finally spoken. It did something smaller and more astonishing. It let the light find them between the trees for a few breaths longer than it should have—enough to make out the faintest crescent carved at shoulder height on a birch, weathered nearly smooth by time and rain.

A sign left by someone who had once trusted him to read signs.

Derwin touched the mark as he passed. "I see you," he said to the birch, to the path ahead, to the girl who had learned how to run without him—and to the woman whose eyes would not forgive quickly.

The day took his words and his resolve, holding them in its quiet, and moved forward without pause, carrying both promise and burden into the hours ahead.

CHAPTER ELEVEN

The forest felt different after a vision like that — as if every branch held its breath to see whether he would break. Even the air seemed heavier, its stillness thick with expectation, like the forest itself was waiting for him to answer a question it dared not speak aloud.

Derwin and Bramble moved slowly, not because the blight pressed closer, but because the weight of what he'd seen made each step deliberate. His body was beginning to betray him in earnest, each injury whispering its own complaint with sharper insistence. Burning beneath their bandages, the bruises along his ribs made breathing a conscious, measured task. Every step sent a dull throb up his leg where a deep cut had begun to stiffen, and his right shoulder ached sharply whenever he shifted the weight of his pack. Even the simple act of keeping his balance felt like a task that drew too deeply from his reserves, forcing him to place each step as though crossing a fragile bridge.

By mid-afternoon, Bramble stopped beside a shallow stream. The water was clear but carried a bitter tang in the air, a reminder of the corruption creeping through the land. Derwin crouched to cup his hands, but when the cold touched his lips, he let it spill away. They would drink later, farther from this place, somewhere the taste of decay didn't linger on the wind.

The stream's bank held a flat patch of ground, sheltered by two leaning alders. It was enough for a camp, and Derwin didn't need more. Lowering his pack, he winced as his shoulder twinged again, the motion pulling at a stitch. His knee threatened to lock if he bent too far, and his hip gave a muted pop that told him the long miles were wearing through more than muscle. He moved with the precision of a man who had learned that careless motions meant torn stitches, reopened wounds, and days stolen from his journey.

He didn't light a fire right away. The quiet was a thing he wanted to measure first. He listened — to Bramble's steady breathing, to the distant creak of tree limbs, to the faint trickle of the stream. Every sound was layered with the ache in his bones, the tension in his jaw, and the slow thud of his heart in his ears. The ache spread beyond his body, settling into the back of his mind where thoughts of Ashling lingered like an old echo.

The memory still pressed against him — Ashling's eyes, Ashling's voice — but here, with no danger, it felt almost bearable. Almost.

He pulled his journal from the pack, a battered leather book more patches than original hide. His charcoal stick was worn to half its length. The first marks he made were only lines, his fingers stiff and trembling, joints reluctant to obey. Then words, slow and uneven:

Ash—

He stared at the single syllable until it blurred. Bramble huffed, shifting his weight, the sound grounding him for a moment. Derwin set the journal aside, rubbing his temples as a dull headache pulsed behind his eyes. The cold was settling in, stiffening his fingers, and the weight of unspoken words hung like frost in the air. The sun dipped lower; shadows stretched. He tried again:

I don't know if this will ever reach you. I don't know if you would want it to.

He hesitated. The ache in his ribs flared when he breathed deep enough to steady himself. His back protested every time he shifted to ease the pain, and the muscles in his legs twitched from fatigue.

I left because I thought it was the only way to keep you safe. I see now it cost you more than it saved. I see it every time I close my eyes.

The words felt too raw, so he smudged them out until the page went gray. One more attempt:

Do you remember the violet thread? You said it would tangle, and it did, but you kept it on anyway. I think about that more than I should.

No more came. He closed the journal without tearing the page.

That night, every time he shifted, a wound reminded him it was still there. The gash on his thigh throbbed in rhythm with his heartbeat. His shoulder stung whenever he turned on his side. His ribs ached with every breath, and the dull pain in his hip made even lying still uncomfortable. His left ankle had begun to swell, forcing him to stretch it every so often just to keep it from locking. The hours came in fragments, broken by Bramble's low rumbles or the scrape of something in the undergrowth. Once, in the deep of night, Derwin woke to find Bramble already standing, ears forward, gaze fixed eastward. Whatever was out there left no sound for human ears, but it left a mark on Derwin's unease.

At dawn, the clouds thinned to a pale gold. Derwin packed in silence, every motion deliberate to avoid pulling at the half-healed cuts. He touched the alder trunk once before mounting Bramble, letting his hand rest against the bark as if drawing strength — or leaving some of his own behind. For a brief moment, he closed his eyes and simply listened to the morning air, wishing he could hold on to this small reprieve.

Derwin lingered in the clearing longer than he planned. The decision was not so much a choice as a necessity—his body made it for him. Each movement reminded him of the fight's cost: deep bruises, ragged cuts, and the stubborn ache in his shoulder where the blighted creature had nearly bowled him over. He cleaned each wound with deliberate care, wincing as cool water bit into the raw skin. The smell of crushed herbs drifted in the air as he ground them into poultices the way Mother Kesa had taught him, hands moving automatically through the motions of a lesson learned long ago.

Bramble stayed close, shifting now and then to watch the forest's edge, ears flicking at unseen sounds. His steady presence was a quiet balm in itself. Derwin noticed how the great beast's breathing seemed to match his own when they rested, a small, unconscious tether keeping him grounded.

By midday, Derwin tested his weight on his legs and wandered the edge of the clearing, gathering edible shoots and roots. The act of foraging slowed him, made him listen—each rustle in the brush, each trill of a bird. His steps took him to a shallow stream where he crouched and tried his hand at fishing, more for the familiarity of the task than hunger. The fish outwitted him, slipping away from his tired hands, but the cool water eased the swelling in his fingers.

It was then that a flash of movement caught his eye. A young doe emerged from between the trees—whole, unblighted, cautious. She froze when she saw him, nostrils flaring, head tilted in wary judgment. Derwin did not move closer, only crouched lower, meeting her gaze without force. The doe took a hesitant step forward, then another, as if testing the air between them. For a moment, it seemed she might come within reach, but a distant crack of a branch sent her bounding back into the green. Still, the moment stayed with him—a reminder of the balance still left to protect.

As evening came, he settled back at the small fire, rewrapping his shoulder and setting the gathered herbs to dry. The forest sang softly around him, unhurried, and he let himself match its rhythm. Bramble's eyes reflected the firelight like two patient embers. Tomorrow they would move again, but for now, Derwin let the quiet have him. In that stillness, his thoughts strayed to the unfinished letter tucked in his pack—a letter meant for Ashling, the words hesitant, unsure, but waiting. He wondered if he would ever find the courage to finish it.

Chapter Twelve

The rain found them first.

It wasn't a storm so much as a persistent mist that thickened, beading on Bramble's fur and soaking the edges of Derwin's cloak. They took shelter beneath a low crown of willow and alder where the ground rose into a shallow mound. The place felt almost chosen—roots braided like a cradle, water sliding away into mossy channels. Derwin eased himself down with a tight breath and set his pack between two knotted roots.

Bramble stood sentry at the open side of the thicket, head tilted, nostrils twitching. The beast didn't growl. He rarely did unless something was wrong. But his stillness was a warning all its own.

"Not far," Derwin murmured. "Whatever it is."

Time slipped. Rain tapped softly overhead. Derwin used it, unwrapping his shoulder to clean the angry seam of the wound. The salve Mother Kesa had given him—what little remained—cooled the heat and banished the worst of the stiffness. He retied the binding slowly, fingers sure despite the ache.

It came as a sound too small for a place this large: a thin, rasping whine.

Bramble's head snapped left. Derwin held up a hand, listening. The sound came again—a struggling breath, then a tiny cough. Not a predator. Not a threat. Something young.

"Easy," he told the beast. "Together."

They moved in a slow curve through the dripping brush, Derwin letting Bramble set the pace. A tangle of windfallen branches formed a low arch, and beneath it lay a small shape the color of damp leaves.

A fox kit.

Its fur should have been bright cinnamon, but corrupt shadows webbed the coat in dull gray-green patches that crawled toward the skin like spilled ink. One leg shook with a fevered tremor. Its eyes—too wide, too glassy—fixed on Derwin and went still with a terror that had nothing to do with him.

"I know," he said softly, dropping to a crouch. "I know."

The kit tried to shrink farther into the wood-pile, but the movement sent a spasm through its body. It keened, a small, broken sound.

Bramble lowered himself to his knees and then to his belly, making his massive frame small—a gesture Derwin had never seen before and would not forget.

Derwin set his staff aside, palms open. He didn't reach, not at first. The last fox he approached had run—torn between instinct and the unnatural stillness the blight imposed. This one couldn't run. He let it see him breathe. In. Out. Slow.

"I won't touch you unless you ask me to," he whispered.

A thin ribbon of drool hung from its jaw and trembled with each breath. Derwin felt the familiar coil of helplessness knotting under his ribs—the one that told him his hands were not enough, that his magic was a frayed rope.

He set about the practical. He cleared the fallen sticks to widen the cradle without jarring the kit. He laid his cloak across the roots to lift the little body off the cold. Bramble tipped his head, shadowing the space with his antlers, sheltering them from the persistent mist.

"Mother Kesa would tell me to start with what I know," Derwin said, mostly to steady himself. He checked for other wounds: a scored paw, a scraped ear, a shallow puncture along the ribs—likely where a thorn had pierced skin already weakened by corruption. He cleaned what he could, breath hissing between his teeth when the kit shuddered.

The blight's stain pulsed under his fingers.

"Not yours," he murmured to the fox. "Not your fault."

The kit blinked, slowly. Its eyes rolled, fighting the heat that wanted to keep them closed. Derwin took the smallest sip from one vial of water and tipped a drop onto its tongue. Another. Another. The throat worked—barely—but it worked.

He had done all he knew to do.

He hovered on the edge of everything else.

"Don't force it," Kesa would say. "Ask."

He placed one hand against the roots and one hand a breath above the kit's ribcage, feeling the small, uneven lift of each breath in the air between them.

"Forest," he said quietly, the word smaller than a prayer. "If there is a way—if I am not meant to be only witness—show me."

Nothing answered—no sudden surge, no warming thread of power. Only rain. Only Bramble's steady breath.

But in the quiet, another sound arrived: a memory, crisp as the day it was made.

A long-ago afternoon in the grove.

He had been younger, not yet a teacher in anything but eagerness. The older druids argued that morning—voices tight, names thrown, histories used like stones. Derwin stood at the edge, hands in his sleeves, wishing himself invisible.

Mother Kesa found him by the mushroom beds, where he had retreated to count caps and not be counted himself.

"You are hiding," she said.

"I'm… reorganizing."

She sat beside him. "Do you know why I want you to teach the little ones?"

"Because I spend too much time with them already?" he offered.

"Because you remember how to be small." She tapped the brim of a stubborn mushroom that refused to unfurl. "This one will not be pushed. It will open when the weight above shifts."

"I'm not…" he gestured vaguely at the arguing elders, "I don't have what they have."

"No," she said, smiling. "You have what they lost. You know how to hold a space until it's safe to open."

She placed his hands around a bowl of water. "Hold. Don't stir. Don't speak. Invite."

They waited, and the surface stilled. The mushroom, unbothered for once by the world's noise, began to unfurl.

Derwin breathed in, then out. He let the space between his palm and the fox be what Kesa had taught him to hold—a bowl that did not spill, a quiet that did not crow its own importance. The ache in his ribs receded to the edges of the moment. Even the rain hushed, or else he simply stopped hearing it.

The air warmed a fraction. The kit's breaths came a little easier, each inhalation less jagged than the last.

He risked lowering his hand until his fingers just brushed the kit's fur. A heat prickled through his palm—not the unpleasant fever-heat of infection, but a tempered warmth that seemed to rise from the contact and then pass through him into the roots beneath. The sensation was so gentle it could have been imagined.

"Easy," he whispered, to himself as much as to the fox.

Bramble exhaled a long, low breath that rippled the mist around them.

Derwin did not call for power. He did not seek a phrase or shape an old word. He simply held the space and let himself be conduit: the breath of a creature in pain, the patient press of living wood, the arc of rain that connected leaf to leaf to ground.

Something gave.

It felt like a knot loosening somewhere small and essential. The gray-green stain along the kit's ribs stopped crawling. The fever heat subsided a degree. The tremor in the leg quieted to an occasional twitch.

Derwin didn't notice he'd been crying until a tear cooled on his jaw.

"Thank you," he said to the roots, "to whatever listened."

The kit blinked again—clearer, slower. It lifted its head, wavered, and then lowered it back to the cloak. A small sound escaped it, not a whine this time, but the tiniest huff. Derwin saw the color return—faint, not more than a breath of cinnamon at the edges of the fur, but there.

He didn't try to do more. He dared not.

He wrapped the kit in the corner of his cloak and tucked the bundle between two roots where the earth held its own steady warmth. He left a palm there, close but not pressing, and at last he let go of the breath he'd been holding.

Bramble shifted and nosed the bundle. The fox did not flinch; it slept.

Rain eased to a fine silver and then to nothing.

Birdsong returned—two notes, then four, then a thread of melody woven from some hidden bough.

Derwin leaned back against the willow and closed his eyes. Fatigue soaked him like the rain, seeping into muscle and thought. Yet a quiet brightness ran beneath it, like veins of light where he'd expected only stone.

He slept.

He woke to Bramble's chin on his knee and the pale color of afternoon bleeding into evening. The kit still slept. The stain along its ribs had retreated to an island the size of a thumbprint.

"Forest be kind," he murmured, and for once the phrase did not feel like a hope too large for his mouth.

Hunger arrived all at once. He ate what he'd gathered: bitter shoots, a handful of sour berries, a strip of dried root from the pack. He brewed a thin tea from a curl of bark and a scatter of mint—more ritual than medicine, more warmth than flavor. Steam rose in whispers and vanished in the damp air.

When the kit woke, it did so with a small sneeze and an offended look, as if the world had stolen its nap. It tried to stand, wobbled, and sat again. Derwin hid his smile
behind the cup.

"Not yet," he advised. "Another hour."

The fox made a noise that was almost a chirp and put its head back down.

The quiet held. Derwin took up his journal.

He did not try to write Ashling's name this time. He began with the thing he could name.

Fox kit, he wrote, and paused to underline the words. *Blight rolled back. No chant. No shaped magic. Holding only. Breathing only. Like the bowl.* His hand hovered. *Like the day Kesa found me in the mushroom beds.*

Charcoal dust deepened in a spot where the stick lingered too long.

Another memory followed on the first, unbidden but welcome now that his fear no longer choked off that passage.

A lesson at dusk, years ago.

Kesa stood with him at the teaching circle while the smallest students chased fireflies that had just begun to blink above the grasses.

“You fear the shape of things,” she’d said.

“I fear breaking them,” he admitted.

“Then practice holding.” She placed a seed in his palm and covered his hand with hers. “Life answers the kind of listening that does not demand.”

He’d felt it then—the tiniest tremor under his skin—as if the idea of a sprout had brushed the idea of his blood and found it agreeable.

“Teach them this,” Kesa said, nodding toward the circle of stumps. “Not to force, but to attend. You are not a hammer, Derwin. You are a hearth.”

Derwin looked up from the journal. Bramble had turned his head toward the east, ears angled like cupped hands. Somewhere far past the trees, the light dimmed in a way that had nothing to do with clouds.

“Tomorrow,” Derwin told the beast. “We’ll move tomorrow.”

He cleaned his tools. He checked each bandage. He set the salves where he could reach them in the dark. The small tasks quieted the mind like smooth stones placed upon a cloth to keep it from lifting in a draft.

When true night came, he lit only a finger-wide flame cupped under his palm and let it go when the heat grew greedy.

The kit woke again, more alert. It stood, this time holding. It took two steps, then three, then stretched with a kittenish yawn that showed a row of tiny clean teeth. The blight's island had shrunk again, now no larger than a seed.

"Go on," Derwin said, and moved his arm so the cloak fell away.

The fox looked toward the woods, then back at him, then toward Bramble, who pretended not to be watching. It took a cautious hop from root to root and disappeared into the brush with a whisper of leaves.

Derwin sat with the absence.

He wished for a moment that someone else had seen it. Kesa's lined hands; Maelin's wide grin; Genn's irreverent whistle. Proof that he had not imagined the loosening of the knot, the warmth between palm and root. Proof that he was not only witness.

Bramble pressed his forehead gently into Derwin's shoulder and held it there.

"That will do," Derwin said, and covered Bramble's brow with his hand.

They slept in turns, under a quilt of willow-shadow and starlight that unstitched itself and restitched as clouds passed.

At dawn the clearing smelled green and faintly sweet—the way moss does after a long drink. Dew limned every blade of grass. A thrush tried three notes, forgot the fourth, and made do.

Derwin rolled his shoulder. The pain had settled into a manageable ember. He unwound the binding from his thigh and found the angry red softened to pink. He flexed his fingers and felt strength answer, not fully, but enough. Even the deep ache in his ribs had fallen from a shout to a persistent murmur.

He wasn't healed. But he was no longer only broken.

He set the journal on the root again and added one line beneath last night's entry: *If rot can spread, so can mercy.*

Then he closed the book, tucked it away, and rose.

They broke camp with the quiet competence of two souls who had shared enough dawns to require few words. Cloak, pack, staff. A careful pat where the fox had slept, as if to seal the place against what waited beyond the trees.

Before they left, Derwin stood under the willow and, without thinking, bowed his head. Not a prayer. Not an oath. A thank you.

Bramble stepped close enough that Derwin could use his shoulder to mount without warning his ribs. The beast accepted the weight with no shift that might jar him.

They took the path east, through dew and dapple and the faint promise of heat.

A hundred paces in, Derwin glanced back.

Something small and bright watched from the underbrush—the

fox kit, or its kin, or the idea of it carried forward. It gave a quick, bobbing nod—nonsense, a trick of leaves—and vanished.

Derwin breathed out and let the forest fill his lungs.

He did not know how he cured the kit—not truly, not in words he could repeat. But a new thread wound through him now, thin and sure, tying him to what he had almost forgotten how to trust.

The day's work waited. The blight's work would not rest. Neither would he.

They moved on, and somewhere behind them, birdsong followed.

Chapter Thirteen

The morning light filtered through the canopy in thin, shifting blades. It painted Bramble's antlers gold as Derwin led him down a narrow trail, the kind that looked like it was made by deer hooves but carried the faint scent of rain-softened moss instead of prey. The forest was calm, but Derwin's thoughts weren't. The memory of the fox kit lingered like an ember in his chest — warm and sharp all at once. He had work to do, places to reach before the blight tightened its grip further.

The sound reached him before the sight did — a muffled thump, followed by a burst of laughter.

He froze.

Not the guttural rasp of a predator, not the hollow echo of blight-stilled things. This was… lighter. Human. Familiar.

"I swear I heard something this way!" a voice called out, full of unearned confidence.

Derwin closed his eyes. "No," he muttered to himself. "Not them."

But the underbrush ahead shook, and two figures stumbled into the clearing — Lira, her braids tied back with what looked like a scrap of bright cloth, and Genn, grinning like he'd just caught a fish with his bare hands or discovered a lost city.

"Found him!"

"This is not 'finding,'" Derwin said. "This is following. And you're supposed to be anywhere but here."

"Supposed to," Lira said with a shrug, "but we figured you'd need help. Or company. Or both."

"I don't need—"

"You always say that," Genn cut in, brushing a leaf from his shoulder. "And every time, you end up nearly dying and someone has to drag you home."

Bramble snorted as if in agreement. Derwin gave him a betrayed look.

"See? Even Bramble's on our side," Lira said, stepping closer.

Derwin started walking again, hoping momentum would shake them off. "Go back."

They followed anyway, boots crunching in rhythm with his steps. "No," Genn said.

It should have been infuriating. And it was, a little. But somewhere under the irritation was something else — the faint hum of being seen, and the sharper edge of knowing these two wouldn't just let him disappear into the trees alone.

"You're going to slow me down."

"We're fast," Lira replied. She stretched out her palm, and a faint ripple of magic shimmered above it — a tether of warm light that danced and curled before fading.

"Who taught you that?" Derwin asked.

"You did," she said with a smirk, "a long time ago. You just didn't notice because you were too busy pretending you weren't teaching."

Genn added, “Also, we’ve been practicing while you’re off brooding in the woods. We’re stronger than you think.”

Derwin studied them. They weren’t lying. There was a steadiness in the way Lira’s magic held, a balance in Genn’s stance that hadn’t been there before. Still…

“This isn’t a game,” he said quietly.

“No,” Genn agreed. “But neither is what’s waiting for you out here. So maybe stop pretending you’re the only one willing to stand in front of it.”

Derwin exhaled through his nose, a sound that wasn’t quite surrender but wasn’t refusal either. “And when you get hurt?”

“Then,” Lira smiled in a way that almost hurt to look at, “you drag *us* home.”

They fell into step beside him, chatting about nothing and everything — the way the squirrels in the north grove had started stealing buttons, the smell of Maelin’s latest attempt at stew, how Bramble had once pretended to sleep so a crow would land on his antlers.

They hadn’t gone far before a stretch of the trail darkened from the blight. It spread like a smear of old ink, curling around roots and bleeding into the groundcover.

“Stay close,” Derwin said automatically.

A shallow creek blocked their way ahead, but the water was wrong — sluggish, with a sheen of green-black oil that caught the light in sickly colors. In the center, a vine-like growth coiled from bank to bank, pulsing faintly.

"Lovely," Genn said, crouching for a better look.

Derwin moved to stop him, but Lira had already knelt beside the water, her eyes narrowing. "I think I can undo that tangle."

"Not without—" Derwin began, but she was already weaving a shape with her hands, a lattice of soft light that mirrored the curve of the vine.

"Pull when I say," she told Genn.

To Derwin's surprise, they worked in perfect rhythm — Lira's magic loosening the vine's grip while Genn, quick and sure, hauled it free in one piece. They tossed it onto the bank, where it withered in the open air. The water began to move again, faintly, almost gratefully.

Derwin looked at them for a long moment. "Where did you learn that?"

"You," Genn said simply, wiping his hands.

That night, they camped near a fallen oak whose hollow trunk made a windbreak. The fire was small by Derwin's insistence, just enough to take the edge off the chill.

When Genn fell asleep with his back against Bramble's flank and Lira lay tracing constellations with her fingertip, Derwin sat alone for a while, his charcoal stick poised over the page.

He didn't write a letter. Not yet. But he wrote their names in the journal, and beneath them: *I never planned to bring them here. But they came anyway. And maybe... that's the point.*

Later that night, a branch cracked in the distance. Derwin was instantly awake, hand on his staff, but the sound didn't repeat. The forest felt… attentive. Not hostile, but not idle either. He stayed on watch longer than planned, eyes scanning the dark.

Lira's quiet voice startled him. "You don't sleep much, do you?"

"Not when others are with me."

She came to sit beside him, holding a scrap of paper and charcoal. "I sketched something. It's terrible, but… here."

She passed it over. In the pale firelight, Derwin saw a rough drawing of himself and Bramble — not heroic, not idealized, just… them. Sitting much as they were now.

"I wanted to remember it," she said softly. "You looking like you belong out here. Like the forest wants you in it."

He didn't know what to say, so he folded the paper carefully and tucked it into his journal.

Near dawn, Genn took his turn at watch. He didn't speak for a long time, just stared into the faint glow of the fire. Finally, he said, "You push people away because you think it keeps them safe."

Derwin didn't answer.

"But sometimes," Genn continued, "it just makes them feel like you don't trust them. Or worse, like you don't want them there."

Derwin let out a long breath. "I've seen what happens when the forest takes someone you can't protect."

"Yeah," Genn said quietly. "And we've seen what happens when you try to fight it alone."

Neither spoke after that, but the silence felt… less like a wall.

When they broke camp, Derwin led the way, still unsure if he'd made the right choice letting them stay — but certain of one thing: they weren't going anywhere.

And maybe, for the first time in a long while, that didn't feel like a mistake.

But as they followed the deer path east, Bramble kept pausing, ears swiveling toward the north.

The air was shifting — faint, but enough for Derwin to taste it on the back of his tongue. A bitterness, like water left in a copper cup too long.

Lira slowed beside him. "Do you feel that?"

He nodded once. "Blight. Not close, but not far enough."

Even as they walked on, the undergrowth seemed to lean away from that direction, and the birdsong thinned until only the creak of branches filled the spaces between their footsteps.

Derwin didn't say it out loud, but the thought lodged behind his ribs all the same: whatever lay ahead was moving toward them, too.

Chapter Fourteen

The forest narrowed into a throat of thickets and low branches, a corridor of bramble and alder where sound went to hide. They followed the faint copper tang in the wind all morning, and now the taste grew strong enough to sting the back of the tongue.

"Stay close to me," Derwin said without turning. "Feet soft. Ears open."

Genn matched his steps, eyes scanning the ground ahead. Lira walked a pace behind, palms open, ready to shape light if she had to. Bramble ghosted to their right, his antlers brushing leaves that seemed unwilling to touch him.

They moved through a patch of fern where the fronds had curled in on themselves, as if trying to keep something out—or in. Birds had gone silent. Even the beetles sounded careful.

Derwin felt the first tug before he saw anything: a pressure in his chest, the kind that often preceded a vision. Not now, he told the forest, and the pulse receded like a wave drawn back before it broke.

A whisper of air. A click.

"Down!" Derwin grabbed Genn's cloak and shoved him forward just as a thorn-twined dart hissed through where the boy's neck had been. It struck the trunk behind them and stuck, the wood blackening where it kissed the bark.

Bramble lunged, putting his body between the children and the trees. Lira's hands lit with a thin ribbon of warm light that curved across Derwin's chest and into the brush, making a soft barrier that turned the next dart into ash.

“Ambush,” Genn breathed, crouched, eyes alive.

“Not at me,” Derwin said through his teeth. Another dart sliced the air and took a line of hair from Lira’s braid. “At you.”

The third dart struck Bramble’s shoulder and snapped in two as if it hit stone. The beast rumbled with something deeper than Derwin had heard before—a warning drawn from a chest built to hold the weight of mountains.

Shapes moved in the brush. Cloaked figures, bark-colored and low, their faces veiled by woven thorns. Dark druidlings—acolytes, perhaps. Or hired hands who’d learned just enough to be dangerous.

“Back to back,” Derwin said. “Bramble—”

The beast was already there, hunching low so the children could press against his flank. Derwin set his staff across his body and breathed once, the way Kesa taught him when panic had eaten his ribs from the inside out. Roots listen best when you breathe as one of them.

A figure surged from the left. Derwin turned and met him with the staff, wood on wood as the attacker swung a cudgel laced with vine. Derwin pushed, twisted, and used the man’s momentum to throw him past; the cudgel cracked against a tree and the vine writhed, trying to bite.

Two more came from the right, aiming low where Lira and Genn crouched. Derwin moved to intercept—and saw the line of a thorn-sling arc toward Lira’s throat.

“Lira!” Genn threw himself in front of her; the thorn grazed his sleeve and sliced a neat red line across his arm. He didn’t show any sign of hesitation—just smiled as he fell from the blow.

“You’re supposed to duck,” Lira hissed, dragging him behind Bramble as she flung a lattice of light toward the slinger. The lattice hit like a net made of warm air; the figure stumbled back, his legs momentarily tangled in nothing.

Derwin saw all of it at once—their fear, their stubbornness, the calculation in the silhouettes moving to flank the children. And something inside him shifted. The anger wasn’t a flame; it was a pressure, slow and crushing. How dare they.

The next attacker rushed him with a hooked blade meant for snagging limbs. Derwin stepped into the man’s guard, shoulder-first, slammed the staff up under his wrist, and heard the clean click-pop of a tendon complaining. The blade fell. Derwin kicked it away.

More shapes. Too many.

He needed space.

Without thinking, he drove the end of his staff into the soil and whispered a word he had not used in years.

The ground answered—hesitant, then willing.

Shoots erupted in a hissing circle around them, the baby-green of new growth flashing to a darker hue in a heartbeat. They weren’t thick enough to hold, not really, but they surprised the attackers, made their feet unsure, and sometimes surprise is more defense than a wall.

“Genn,” Derwin said, eyes forward. “Left side. Aim low.”

“What am I—”

“Your sling.”

Genn blinked, then fumbled for the leather loop at his belt—the one he kept mostly for skipping stones. He wound, released, and a pebble snapped into the shin of a druidling with such honest force the figure folded.

"You taught me this," Genn said, delighted.

"You insisted I did," Derwin muttered, and knocked aside another strike.

A dark chant rose from the brush—thin, reedy voices that scraped the air raw. The thorns in the darts began to pulse, the same sickly rhythm Derwin had felt in the totems. Lira's light flickered under it.

"Don't match their rhythm," Derwin said. "Find your own. Think of the river at dusk."

Lira closed her eyes, inhaled, and when she exhaled, the ribbon stilled. It didn't shine brighter. It grew steadier, and the next volley of thorns turned to dust against it.

Bramble placed his massive body where the blows should land. An acolyte misjudged the distance and found an antler under his ribs; the breath whooshed from him and he crumpled like parchment.

Derwin pivoted to follow the next threat—too late. A hooked blade slipped past his guard and bit into his side. Heat flashed; the world narrowed; the old injury's memory screamed louder than the new.

He did not fall. He planted his feet and let the pain become a beach for the wave to break on.

"Derwin!" Lira's voice stretched thin.

“I’m here,” he said, and meant it.

He saw the attacker’s eyes—young, frightened, almost apologetic. The boy glanced beyond Derwin toward Genn. That was the true target. Rage rose again, a tide that wanted to pull him under, to make his hands dumb and heavy wanting to hurt.

No.

Derwin shifted, caught the hook with his staff, slid forward into the boy’s space, and pressed his palm to the bark-stitched cuirass over the boy’s heart. “Sleep,” he whispered.

The old magic answered through him like a memory of sunlight on closed eyes. The boy sagged. Derwin let him down gently and turned to the next.

The thicket to their right exploded with motion—three acolytes at once, coordinated and quiet. Bramble lowered his head and drove forward like a boulder deciding it had had enough of a hill. Derwin flowed in to guard the opening he knew that push would make. Genn slid where he pointed, slinging stones, a rhythm now, grin fading into something like focus. Lira anchored the line with her steady thread of light.

For a few heartbeats, they worked like a single thought.

Then came the second chant.

It scraped lower, nearer to the ground, and the vines themselves began to crawl. New thorns sprouted from old, seeking ankles, wrists, whatever they could drink from. A totem had to be near—something feeding the spell.

“Find the root,” Derwin said, breath ragged. “It’s anchoring somewhere—”

"I see it," Lira said, pointing with her chin. Twenty paces back, half-hidden under a drooping crown of fern, a knotted tangle of bone and bark pulsed faintly. It looked like a nest that had forgotten what it was for.

"Genn," Derwin said, meeting the boy's eyes. "Can you hit that?"

"Bet me," Genn said, already winding. A thorn-studded dart skimmed his cheek; he didn't flinch. He released. The stone struck the totem with a clean, ringing tock.

The chant faltered. The vines stuttered.

Bramble took the opening and leapt, an impossible surge for something so large, his hooves finding a path between roots as if he had always known it. He landed beside the totem and brought an antler down like a hammer.

The bone knot split. The pulse went out like a candle pinched between fingers.

Silence didn't fall, it thrust itself upon their shoulders. The acolytes hesitated—children in masks, almost all of them, their courage borrowed and now overdue.

"Run," Derwin said—not to his own, but to the ones who had come to kill them. "You made your choice. Make a better one."

Two fled at once, crashing through fern. Another lingered, shaking, and then followed.

The last one didn't. He raised a small iron whistle to his mouth and blew.

No sound. Not for human ears.

It hit Bramble first. The beast reeled, eyes going wide, a wounded sound crawling up his throat. Derwin's heart slammed. He hurled his staff; it cracked the whistle from the acolyte's mouth and the boy toppled.

But the damage was done. The whistle hadn't called help—it had woken what slept beneath the thorns.

The brush behind them heaved. A shape pulled itself free from the ground: something that had once been a stag, its antlers braided with wire vine, its eyes slick with the same red dimness Derwin had fought before. Its breath came with a bubbling hiss; black sap bled from a split along its spine.

"Stay behind Bramble," Derwin said, voice low. "Do not run."

The creature charged.

Derwin stepped into it, because there was no other way. He slid to the right at the last moment, staff arcing, catching the corrupted jaw. The shock rang through his arms. Lira's light flared to mark the ground where the beast's feet would land; the stag stumbled around the brightness, a fraction slower. Genn pelted its knees with stones until the joints snarled.

"Roots," Derwin whispered, and felt the earth answer with a weary willingness. Vines rose and wrapped the stag's left foreleg. It tore free, but the pause was enough for Bramble to shoulder in, antlers locking with the stag's broken crown.

They pushed.

Bramble's muscles bunched like cables. The stag twisted, plant-wire sawing over Bramble's hide, drawing sap and blood together. Derwin darted in, struck the joint, felt the crunch, heard the stag scream.

A jag of vine whipped from the stag's back, catching Derwin across the ribs exactly where the hooked blade had bit him. Stars burst white. His knees went watery. For a breath, the world narrowed to the wet hot of pain and the taste of copper.

It would be so easy to give the anger the reins. To pull, hard, at the part of him that could turn roots to shackles and thorns to teeth. To hurt until hurt stopped happening to the people behind him.

"No," he told himself and the forest. "Not like them."

He adjusted his grip. He waited for the half-second between the stag's inhale and its next heave.

"Now," he said, and the word wasn't a command so much as a chord.

Lira dropped her light not on the stag, but over Bramble—an open circle of warmth that gave him a breath that wasn't pain. Genn's next stone struck exactly where Derwin's last blow had softened bone. Derwin drove the staff down, a lever at the joint.

The stag's leg buckled. Bramble heaved and, with a sound like a tree finally giving way after a long wind, threw the corrupted creature onto its side.

"Hold," Derwin said, though his vision swam. He pressed his palm to the ground and reached—for what, he didn't know, only that there had to be something besides destruction.

The answer came like a memory of green. A thread. Thin as spider silk.

He took it.

"Be still," he whispered to the stag—not to the rot crawling through it, but to the thing under the rot, the thing that remembered running without pain. "Be still. Be still."

For a heartbeat, the red dimness in its eyes thinned. A sound came from its chest that might have been a sob.
Derwin felt the thread slip; he had no more to give.

"Derwin—" Lira said.

"I know." He stood. He didn't want to. He did anyway. He raised the staff.

"I'm sorry," he told the stag, and meant it.

The staff came down. The corrupted neck gave with a wet crack. The stag stilled.

Silence came, but it wasn't clean. It carried the echoes of what they'd done and what they hadn't been able to do.

Derwin staggered. His side burned in pulses that felt out of time with his heart. The world listed; the trees tilted and corrected.

Genn was suddenly under his arm, all wiry strength and stubbornness. "I've got you."

"Shelter," Derwin said. "We need—" He swallowed. Black dots chased each other at the edge of his vision. "We need out of the open."

Bramble nudged him from the other side, careful, the way he had when Derwin bled against his fur days ago. Lira moved ahead, scanning, then pointed. "There. Rock overhang. Dry."

They half-walked, half-stumbled into the shallow cave the roots

had carved beneath the rise. It smelled of dust and old leaves. Genn eased Derwin down against the wall; Bramble took the entrance, body filling the space with the absolute suggestion that nothing was coming
through unless invited.

Lira's hands shook as she unbuckled Derwin's belt to get at the bandage, but her voice didn't. "Talk to me."

"Cut from before," Derwin said, jaw clenched. "Reopened."

She peeled the fabric back. The wound looked angrier than it had any right to—raw, edges bruised where the vine had snapped across it. "You're lucky," she said softly. "It missed deeper muscle."

"Feels like it didn't," he managed, and she huffed a laugh despite herself.

Genn pressed a folded cloak into Derwin's hands. "Bite it if you have to."

"I'm not biting—" Derwin started, then hissed as Lira poured clean water over the wound. He bit the cloak.

They worked fast. Lira ground feverfew and yarrow with the butt of her knife, her motions sure. Genn held the edges of the wound together with hands that didn't shake, despite being twelve and stubborn and terrified. Derwin breathed and watched the curve of Bramble's spine as the beast breathed with him.

"Almost," Lira said. "On three."

"Just do it," Derwin said through his teeth.

She did. The poultice hit like fire and then, blessedly, like cool earth. She wrapped him in clean linen, tight enough to make his heartbeat louder in his ears.

When she finished, she sat back on her heels and wiped her hands on her trousers, leaving green smudges. Genn didn't move until Derwin nodded. Then he sat down hard and let his head tip back against the rock.

The cave was very quiet. Outside, the wind shifted, carrying the smell of crushed fern and iron from the fight.

Derwin swallowed and found his voice. "You were good," he said to both of them. "More than good."

Genn shrugged without looking over. "You told us to stay behind Bramble. We did."

"Mostly," Lira added, lips twitching. Then her face sobered. "They were after us."

"Yes." Derwin stared at the slow drip of water at the cave mouth. "That's what I hate most."

"They'll try again," Genn said, not as fear, but fact.

"Yes," Derwin said again, and this time he let the anger surface where they could both see it. "And I will be there when they do."

Lira leaned her shoulder into his arm as if to anchor him. "We all will."

Bramble huffed, a low sound that might have been agreement. He flicked one ear toward the woods, then relaxed, the set of his weight in the entrance changing from fight-ready to watchful rest.

Derwin closed his eyes. For a moment, he let the cave hold them. He let the ache be honest. He let the fight settle into his bones the way old storms sometimes do, their electricity taking a while to leave the air.

He had not fought perfectly. He had fought right enough to keep them alive. There would be a cost for that—the forest always tallied—but for now, the debt could wait its turn.

"Sleep," he said, and when neither of the children moved, he added, softer, "That's an order."

They obeyed. Genn's breathing evened out quickly, the boy burning through adrenaline into exhaustion. Lira lasted longer, eyes open in the dark, but when Derwin shifted and winced and she saw he wasn't breaking, her lids lowered too.

Only Derwin and Bramble stayed awake. The beast's breath was a slow bellows. Outside, the bruise of land beyond the trees waited, patient as rust.

Derwin rested a hand over the fresh bandage and whispered to the roots under the rock, the way a man might speak to an old friend he'd offended and hoped to make amends with.

"Tomorrow," he said. "I'll listen better tomorrow."

The forest did not answer. But somewhere under the slow pulse of his pain, he felt it remember him.

CHAPTER FIFTEEN

The rain began sometime before dawn. A light downpour. Long, patiently sifting through the leaves in a way that made the forest smell older, deeper. Derwin woke to it and to the quiet weight of Bramble's presence at the cave mouth. The beast hadn't moved all night except to turn his head when the wind shifted, listening to things only he could hear.

The children were curled in their cloaks, Genn's arm flung across his face, Lira's fingers still faintly glowing in her sleep as if she had been guarding even in dreams. Derwin's side throbbed where the bandage pressed, but it was a duller ache now, more a reminder than a threat.

He rose carefully, mindful not to wake them, and stepped to the edge of the overhang. The forest beyond seemed to hold its breath. Every drip from the canopy rang clear.

"Still here," he murmured to the trees.

They didn't answer, but the roots under his boots shifted—in a subtle way, as if a vast presence had turned its head.

They moved slowly that morning. Derwin insisted on it. His injury was a ready excuse, but truthfully, he wanted the forest to decide what it would show them. Rushing only made it close its doors.

The forest stretched ahead in dappled, shifting light, each patch of sun breaking through the canopy like a fleeting promise. The air was heavy with damp earth and the faint metallic tang that always seemed to precede blighted ground. Derwin led the way, Bramble's hooves sinking quietly into the moss, while the children walked on either side, their eyes darting between the familiar and the strange. The blight was quieter here, though not gone. Vines still bore the slick black gloss, and the air still had that faint tang of copper, but the plants seemed to be… listening. Waiting.

The terrain changed slowly but noticeably — soft forest loam giving way to root-tangled ridges where ancient trees leaned like old sentinels keeping reluctant watch. Shafts of gold light would filter through for moments, only to be swallowed by the deep greens and shadow again. They crossed a small stream, its clear water reflecting the shifting light overhead, and Derwin paused to fill their flasks. He let the children go ahead, watching them as they leaned in together, whispering about what they'd do if they ever caught sight of the dark druid himself. By midday they reached a stretch where the path narrowed between two massive oaks whose roots arched like the ribs of a great beast. Derwin stopped beneath them, pressing a palm to the wood. He felt the whisper then—a tremor moving up through his arm, as if the tree had spoken into his bones.

The day unfolded in slow, deliberate steps. They stopped at an old stump, scarred from lightning long ago, and Derwin used it as a place to explain the way trees could survive after losing their crowns. Genn ran his fingers along the grooves, imagining the storms it had endured. Lira asked if the blight could be weathered the same way, and Derwin had no easy answer. A vision came, quick and sharp: a flash of the dark druid grove in full, awful bloom. Branches twisting into spires. Masks carved from living bark. And in the center, the faint suggestion of a figure—hooded, watching him. The weight of its attention heavy on Derwin's mind.

Camp that night was made in a hollow beneath an outcropping of stone. The fire popped and hissed as Derwin boiled water for tea while the kids busied themselves with herbs they'd gathered earlier. Once they'd settled, Genn leaned forward. "Derwin," he asked, "when you… when you cleansed that deer, how did you do it? It looked like magic, but it wasn't like the spells we've learned."

"What is it?" Lira asked.

He pulled back, breath misting in the cool air.

Derwin considered, staring into the flames. "It wasn't something I called. It was something I… felt. Like the forest knew I wanted to help and lent me its hands for a moment."

Lira's brow furrowed. "Can you teach us?"

"Not by standing here."

They tried. Derwin gathered them close, guiding them through breathing, focusing on the feel of the earth beneath their palms, the flow of energy as life rather than power. But each attempt failed — the blighted root he'd brought as practice shriveled further. "It's not ready to listen to you yet," he told them, seeing their disappointment. "But it will, if you keep trying."

Later, when the children had gone to sleep, Derwin sat alone, listening to the forest's shifting chorus. The healthy parts spoke in rustles and the occasional distant hoot, but in the blighted stretches, the silence was loud — a pressure on his ears, a constant awareness of something wrong.

His dreams that night were vivid and unsettling. A grove he didn't recognize, lit in pale, green fire. Figures in robes walking among twisted trees. The voice of the forest calling his name, not in warning this time, but something closer to grief. He woke before dawn, breathless, with Bramble staring toward the east.

The next day's travel was slower. They passed through a stand of aspens that quivered unnaturally, their leaves shivering without wind. In the distance, they saw a fox — blighted, but not attacking. It stood watching, eyes glassy yet alert, trembling as though caught between two pulls. Derwin spoke softly to it, his voice carrying the weight of patience. The fox shifted, took a single step forward, then bolted, vanishing into shadow. He watched it go, knowing it was a sign: the creatures wanted to be free, but were bound by something deeper than fear.

Bramble grew restless, ears twitching. Derwin followed his gaze and saw it — a strange totem embedded in a tree, pulsing faintly with corrupted magic. He stepped closer, fingers brushing the surface. It was cold, almost slick, and as his skin met the wood, a jolt of dread swept through him — an echo, the sensation of being watched.

They left it behind, but he carried its shadow in his mind as they pressed on. The forest's whispers followed.

They made camp early, under a low rock ledge where the rain's voice was steady but soft. Genn wandered to gather dry sticks, and Bramble padded after him, antlers scraping against the stone above. Lira settled near Derwin, watching him coax a fire from damp tinder.

"You felt something back there," she said.

Derwin didn't look up. "The forest remembers more than we do. Sometimes it tries to share."

"Does it ever show you the good memories?"

"Once in a while." He smiled faintly, though it didn't reach his eyes. "But it knows I need the warnings more."

That night, Derwin dreamed. Or perhaps he listened. It was hard to tell where one ended and the other began.

He was walking beneath roots, their great pillars descending into a green-lit dark. Whispers wound around him, not in any tongue he knew but in the cadence of water and wind. Shapes moved beyond the roots—antlers, wings, long hands tipped with claws—but none came close. The path curved until it opened on a pool black as polished stone.

Something broke the surface. A hand, pale and bark-veined, holding a seed the color of old gold.

"The seed does not choose the soil," the whispers said together. "But it may cleanse it."

The hand sank. The pool stilled.

Derwin woke with the taste of loam in his mouth.

The next day was harder. The blight thickened without warning, curling over ferns and swallowing fallen logs whole. The ground turned soft, sucking at their boots. Genn kept glancing back at Derwin's side, but the druid waved him on.

By late afternoon, Bramble froze mid-step. His ears swiveled toward the trees ahead, muscles coiled.

"What is it?" Genn whispered.

Derwin listened. At first he heard nothing—then a faint tapping, like claws on bark. Not one set. Many. Circling.

"Keep close," he said. "Eyes up."

The forest around them seemed to dim. Even the rain quieted.

From the shadows between the trees, small shapes emerged—foxes, their fur patchy with blight, eyes clouded but not fully lost. One stepped forward, head low, tail stiff. Derwin crouched slowly, meeting its gaze.

"You don't want this," he murmured. "I can feel it."

The fox flinched, paws shifting. For a heartbeat its eyes cleared, and it let out a sharp, pained yip before spinning and vanishing into the undergrowth. The others followed, leaving only the sound of disturbed leaves.

"They're scared," Lira said softly.

"They're trapped," Derwin corrected. "Scared is just what's left over."

They found shelter in the hollow of an ancient cedar whose trunk split into three. Inside, the air was dry, lined with old moss. Derwin sank against the wall, exhaustion heavy in his bones.

That night, the roots whispered again—but this time, the voice was different. Not the vast, patient tone of the forest, but something thinner. Urgent.

It spoke in images: a shadow crossing water, antlers hung with bone charms, the masked figure from his earlier vision reaching into the soil with both hands.

When Derwin woke, the whisper was still in his ears.

"They're moving," he said to himself. "Closer."

Bramble stirred and looked toward the east, the same way Derwin's thoughts had already turned.

Tomorrow, they would follow.

CHAPTER SIXTEEN

Following the sour pull, Derwin, Bramble, Genn, and Lira stepped into enemy country—where mockery hunts as sharply as fang and claw.

The air changed by degrees, the way a fever slides into a body that was certain it was fine. First the temperature—cooler in the shade of red-needled pines that did not belong here—then the soundscape: birdsong thinned to single notes, then to the creak of bough against bough. Finally, the smell: resin and iron, old smoke and something like wet leather left too long in a cellar. Even the wind felt different, its fingers trailing cold against the nape of Derwin's neck.

Bramble dropped his head and snorted once, slow and heavy. The pulse still ghosted across Derwin's palm like pins-and-needles gone wrong, a dark compass pulling them deeper. He let it lead, because not knowing was worse. In the brief silences between their steps, he thought he could hear a faint ticking—as though the forest itself counted down.

"Stay tight," Derwin said over his shoulder. His voice came out hushed without his intending it. "No wandering. If I stop, you stop."

Genn nodded, jaw squared. Lira walked closer than usual, one hand at Bramble's shoulder, the other at her belt where she carried the charcoal stick and a coil of cord she'd learned to braid from the younger ones. Her glow was a soft pulse under her skin—the forest answering her nerves with its own uneasy light. Genn tried a whisper-joke about her looking like a lantern; Lira managed a small smirk, but her eyes didn't leave the shadows.

They moved through a corridor of trees that leaned inward as if conspiring. Here the blight did not coat so much as thread: fine black filaments etched along veins of leaves, like writing in a language older than the bark. A squirrel darted across their path, fur patchy, tail twitching erratically before it vanished with a squeal into the dark.

“Look,” Lira whispered. Tiny white moths clung to the filaments—alive, but barely, wings half-fused with the sticky black threads. Derwin breathed out slowly and touched the nearest trunk. The moth shivered and pulled free, tottering into the air before spiraling toward a patch of untainted fern. Not a cure—only a kindness—but even that felt like rebellion.

The path ended at a clearing no wider than a house. At its center stood a new totem—a column of bound saplings, bark peeled into ribbons that flapped without wind. Bone charms clicked against each other in a rhythm a little too regular to be chance.

“Don’t touch this one,” Derwin said, stepping between the children and the column. “Let me see it first.”

He circled once. This construct wasn’t anchored like the first; it was aimed. The saplings angled southeast, their exposed rings stained with a dark oil that seeped down into the soil. A trail. A sending.

A crow dropped from the canopy and landed atop the totem. It wore a collar of braided bark. Its eyes were wrong—too reflective, like polished seeds. It opened its beak, but what came out was not a caw.

“Little teacher,” said the crow in a voice that was not a bird’s and not quite a man’s. “You walk my corridors.”

Genn jerked back. Lira grabbed his sleeve.

Derwin lifted his chin, every instinct ordering him not to answer. He answered anyway. "You poison what is not yours."

The crow clicked its beak. Bone charms answered like laughter.

"What is not mine?" the voice purred through the bird. "Soil is vessel. Vessel is use. Use is truth. Your elders taught you prettier lies."

Derwin took another slow step, putting his body where he wanted the children not to be. "If you need a messenger," he said, "you are still afraid to meet."

"Afraid?" The crow's head cocked, and for a heartbeat the bird mimed a human gesture as if shrugging. "Why fear a candle when I carry night? I send a voice because your fear walks with children. It is poor sport to snap saplings before they bend."

Genn flushed. Lira's fingers glowed brighter.

Derwin swallowed his reply. He would not gift the voice their rage. "What do you want?"

"To admire my work." The crow pivoted, beak pointing down the angled saplings. "Follow the line and see where the river takes rot. I am generous with tours."

Derwin felt the tug of the southeast angle again—like a muscle memory he had never learned. "And at the end?"

"At the end," the voice said lightly, "a riddle answers itself. Your grove was lesson one. The settlement you play at mending? Lesson two. I would save you the walk, but I find you learn best from edges."

The clearing tightened around them. Derwin heard his own

heartbeat. He forced his breath steady.

“You won’t touch them,” he said. He didn’t recognize the prayer in his tone until he heard it. “Not while I breathe.”

“Then do not breathe long,” the crow said, almost kindly. It shook, as if in laughter. The bark collar cracked. The bird’s eyes flashed red-gold—Ashling’s ember-glint for the smallest instant—then became only bird again. It took wing.

Bramble leapt. One snap of antler took the totem at its middle. The bound saplings shattered, bone charms skittering through leaves. The ground exhaled, the dark pull lessened—did not vanish.

Derwin crouched. Where the totem had stood, the soil was blackened to the depth of his knuckles. He pressed his palm flat. Heat radiated up, rhythmic—like a pulse.

“Warden lines,” he said, grim. “A net. He’s pushing blight along paths. We followed one in.”

“To… to where?” Genn asked.

Derwin traced the angled stain again. “Back to them. Or forward to what they love.” He met Lira’s eyes. She understood first. Her mouth went thin.

“The settlement,” she whispered.

He stood so fast his vision swam. Bramble bumped his hip to steady him.

“We run,” Derwin said. “But smart. If these lines cross, they’ll trap us in the middle. We go around and cut as many as we can on the way.”

"The crow said you learn from edges," Lira murmured.

Derwin forced a tight smile. "Then we'll make him regret giving us a map."

They moved like hunters who knew they were also hunted—fast when the trees opened, still as stones when the forest held its breath. Derwin felt for the warden lines the way he might once have felt for water beneath river stones: a thrum underfoot, a direction in his bones. Twice Bramble warned them off a stretch that looked clean but rang wrong; both times, a small stretch further on, they found another totem, smaller than the first and hidden in bracken. Once, a blight-warped fox slunk from the brush, muzzle twitching, but it turned aside without challenge, eyes clouded with some inner order.

Derwin taught while he cut. "Not with heat," he told Lira, when she reached for a spark. "Heat wakes it. Cold hands. Steady. Think of roots that will not be hurried." Together they unwound the bindings, scattered bone charms in streams, packed raw earth into the hole. The pulse weakened, then stuttered out. As they worked, Lira asked in a low voice if the crow's words were true about the elders' lies; Derwin's pause before answering was longer than she liked.

Genn learned to listen for the counterfeit wind—how blighted totems made leaves tremble on windless air. He took to smashing the smallest markers with a rock he had christened sensibly, if not poetically, Cracker. Each hit came with a muttered, "For the little ones," and Lira stopped teasing him about the name.

Near sundown they found a crossing of three lines, each marked only by a nail of blood-iron hammered into a living trunk. Derwin cursed under his breath. "King's iron," he said. "Funded, trained…" His throat closed on the thought of letters he had not shown the children.

He placed his hand around the nail and waited. The wood moaned—quiet agony. “I know,” he whispered. “Forgive me.” He pulled. The iron slid free with a sick, wet sound, and sap bled clear around the wound. Lira caught the drop in her cupped hand and pressed her palm to the bark. The glow beneath her skin flowed outward, thin as a thread, a promise of mending if not forgetting.

They made a cold camp in a seam of rock while the sky bruised to indigo. Derwin ate little, every muscle tuned to the forest’s unsung music. Twice in the night the crow’s voice returned, riding different throats—a hare, a jay—always just far enough to make him question direction.

“Little teacher,” it crooned once, too softly to wake the children. “I like your students. The girl bears light like a fruit. The boy, a stubborn root. Snap or graft? I have hands for both.”

Derwin closed his eyes and breathed in through his nose, out through his mouth, until the want to stand and run—now, blindly—subsided to a contained flame. Bramble pressed nearer and did not sleep at all.

Morning broke thin and copper. They cut two more lines before the sun cleared the tallest firs. At the third, Derwin found a tether stone: a black river-rock bound with wire, sigils burned into its face. He crouched, tracing one sigil with a knuckle.

“It’s a channel,” he said. “He pushes through here when he wants the flow to surge. Like opening a sluice.”

Genn frowned. “So close it.”

Derwin set both palms on the stone and let his breath find a rhythm: three heartbeats in, hold for two, four beats out. The sigils warmed under his hands—then cooled. He pressed harder.

The air smelled suddenly of slick, deep water. A voice he did not know—not the crow—murmured as if from far down a well: *Not yours.*

"Watch him," Lira said to Genn, kneeling at Derwin's shoulder.

Derwin kept his palms down. "It isn't mine," he said aloud, surprising himself. "That's why it can't stay."

He pictured the seed from his dream—a pulse of gold in black water—and let that picture move through his hands. Not force. Permission. The sigils dimmed. The wire slackened. The stone went dull as any other river-rock.

Derwin sagged back on his heels. Bramble touched his shoulder with the broad edge of an antler, a steadying, nearly human gesture.

Genn picked up the dead stone and heaved it into a ravine. "Sluice that," he muttered, and for once Derwin did not correct his tone.

By late afternoon, the forest began giving warnings it could not have known how to give when he was younger: a thousand ants evacuating a log in a single quiet sheet; a line of swallows crossing the sky, all turning at once, as if a great invisible shape had brushed them. Bramble's ears never settled.

They reached a slope carpeted in red needles and there found what at first looked like a shrine—circles of smooth stones, a spill of dried berries, three little woven figures set upright in the center. Lira took a step forward, smiling. "Offerings?"

"Bait," Derwin said. He caught her sleeve. "Look at the weave."

The figures were made of the same black filaments they had seen earlier, twined with hair. Child hair, cut close to the scalp. Lira's smile fell away. Genn swore softly and kicked one of the stones. The circle broke like spun glass striking a floor.

The totems did not hum here. They whistled. A high, almost sweet sound just under hearing. Derwin felt it in his teeth.

"Why would he leave these?" Lira whispered.

"To see who will be tender. And to teach them that tenderness hurts." Derwin crouched, hands hovering. "We won't let him own that lesson."

Together they unwove the figures, whispering to the hair as if it could listen. Lira braided it into a single long strand and tied it around a young birch. "Grow tall," she said, voice rough. "Give them back their years."

The whistling stopped.

They cut one last line as the light went blue. Derwin was slow standing afterward, hands shaking with the strain he pretended not to feel. He let himself lean against Bramble longer than pride would have preferred.

"We can make the settlement by dawn," he said finally. "If we don't sleep."

"That's not a plan," Genn said. "That's a prayer."

"Most plans are," Derwin answered, surprised into honesty.

They pushed on. The forest tightened into lanes—old stag paths opening one after another, as if the land itself remembered haste. Derwin did not question the gift. He only ran softer, breathed deeper, trusted the rhythm that had saved him more than he deserved.

Halfway down a narrow draw, the crow's voice came one last time, nearer than before—so near it could have been spoken into the back of Derwin's neck.

"Turn back, little teacher," it whispered. "The lesson writes itself without you."

Derwin stopped. Not because the voice told him to, but because the forest did. Every leaf along the draw stood still. The hair on his arms rose.

"Derwin?" Lira asked quietly.

He lifted a hand. Listened.

For a breath—two—nothing. Then the ground far ahead shivered. Once. A second time, closer. A footfall that did not belong to a single creature.

Bramble's entire body went rigid. His eyes found Derwin's.

Run, the forest said—not in words, but in a chorus of things that had never, until this moment, agreed: ants and birds, roots and wind, stone and animal.

Derwin did not argue.

"Mount," he told the children, voice gone flint. "Now."

Genn scrambled up Bramble's flank. Lira swung behind him. Derwin took the front, fingers already slicking down the leather of the saddle the children made. He did not look back at the woven birch or the broken totems or the red-needle slope. The draw opened into a long, shallow valley, and Bramble dropped into a ground-eating lope he had never shown them before.

The last light died. The first stars shook. Somewhere far behind, something began to sing—a low, collective moan pitched to the key of rot.

Derwin bent to Bramble's neck and whispered, "Faster."

The beast obliged.

CHAPTER SEVENTEEN

They did not make the settlement by dawn.

The beast hunted them deep into the ridgeways, driving them off the stag paths and into gullies no map marked. Bramble's stride held, tireless, but even his lungs could not outrun the thing that sang in the dark. Only when the ground broke into split shale and jagged ridges did the moan finally fade, leaving them hollowed out and half a day's march from anywhere they meant to be.

By the second night, Derwin knew they were days behind. He said nothing to the children, only walked beside Bramble with his hand at the beast's shoulder, measuring each breath against the thought that he led them wrong again.

At dawn on the third day, the forest itself interrupted his shame. The wind carried a sweetness that did not belong here—pitch boiled with honey, smoke without flame. Bramble's ears pinned, and Derwin's stomach turned in the old way, the way it had when he was a boy and the roots first trembled.

They crested a shale slope and looked down.

The land fell away into a shallow bowl where no birds sang, and there it was: a river that was not a river, gray-black and slow, wearing a skin of ash that cracked and shifted as if it breathed, revealing a sheen below like oiled glass. An ash vein. Ancient. Alive.

Derwin stopped, pulse quickening. They had lost days to the beast, but this—this was worth the loss.

"Stay close," he said, voice low. "This is older than us."

The grove's maps had marked some, but always far to the north and listed in the margins as folklore: old wounds the world scabbed over and learned to live around. This one pulsed.

Genn crouched and picked up a pebble. "Don't," Derwin said. Genn froze and let the stone fall from his fingers.

Bramble lowered his head and blew a breath across the bowl. The ash skin dimpled, then smoothed. Even the beast stepped back.

"They built around these," Derwin said, almost to himself. "Or fled them. They didn't make them."

"Who?" Lira asked.

"Whoever came before us," he answered. He didn't mean the druids only.

They skirted the bowl on a path of broken rock and short grass, careful not to slide. At the far edge, the ground rose to a low ridge of stone. Derwin paused and placed his palm against it. The ridge was warm, the way a rock gets warm in summer even on a cold day — radiating a heat that was not the air's. He closed his eyes and listened.

There was a soft, steady thrum that lived somewhere at the base of his skull. It felt like a heartbeat in the wrong place.

"Veins," he murmured. "More than one. Crossing under us."

Lira glanced from his hand to the ridge. "Like roots?"

"Like roots," he said, "if the tree were made of winter."

A narrow cut wound its way down into a shallow ravine ahead, and there the land broke open into a junction of four ash veins meeting, two crossing the ravine and two running with it. Where they intersected, a rise of stone had been shaped by hands a very long time ago into a kind of island: a flat-backed altar no wider than a table, encircled by standing posts worn down to shin-bones by wind and age. Petroglyphs, faint as breath, ringed the stone — spirals, moons, something that might have been a seed or a closed eye.

Derwin stepped down into the ravine and found that his breath fogged, though the morning wasn't cold enough for frost. The air here was thinner, tight in the chest. He felt the old knife's weight at his belt, and the willow-and-copper necklace under his tunic warmed against his skin in a way that wasn't wholly comforting.

"Don't touch anything yet," he said. "Let me listen."

Genn made a face but obeyed, planting himself guard-like at the lip of the ravine. Lira went quiet in the way she did when the world got big inside her; a gentle glow rose under her skin, as if her body remembered sun even when the sky did not.

Derwin circled the altar once, then again, slow enough that the children grew antsy and then remembered patience. He felt for pattern: which way the ash skin cracked and healed; where the wind stumbled; which petroglyphs had been scratched deeper to survive; what moss dared live between the posts. When he knelt and pressed a palm to the stone, a shiver ran up his arm like cold water. He breathed through it.

The vision did not strike so much as settle — like dust in a room you didn't know you'd entered.

A clearing at night. Torches set high and far so the dark between them felt like a living thing. People — not druids as Derwin knew them, but something older. Some wore bark masks, some none at all. They stood without speaking around a shape that might have been a tree and might have been a body, wrapped in layers of reed and cloth. Hands made slow signs over the shape. The air hummed with a note too low to hear.

The wrapped shape convulsed. The note broke. A woman's voice said, "Not from here. Not from now." A man's voice answered, "Then we hold it here until the season learns it."

Derwin's hand jerked back. He knelt harder to keep from falling. Lira touched his shoulder without quite touching.

"What did you see?" she whispered.

"Not ours," he said. His throat was dry. "Older. They knew the veins. They tried to make… barriers. Or bridges. I'm not sure which."

Genn kicked at a stone just to have something solid under his boot. "If they were so old and so wise, why's it all still here?"

"Because the world keeps breathing," Derwin said. "Sometimes in, sometimes out." He pointed at the posts. "And because even good work rots."

He drew the dagger and set it, point down, gently to the altar. The metal didn't flare. It didn't drink or burn. It cooled until the hilt felt cold in his hand.

"What are you?" he asked softly to the place.

The ash skin across the nearest vein broke with a sound like thin ice under a skater's foot. Below, the blackness rippled and showed a light like a firefly trapped in tar. Derwin flinched and then leaned in, as if his body had already decided to be brave.

The light flickered once, twice, then steadied. Intent.

"Do you see that?" Lira breathed.

"Only just," Derwin said. The light did not look malignant. It looked stubborn.

He slid the dagger back into its sheath and took the willow-and-copper necklace from under his tunic. The metal crescents were warm — too warm for the day. He set the largest against the altar and waited. Nothing.

He exhaled and made the smallest of choices: he traced the once-closed eye glyph with the tip of his charcoal stick until the shape was whole again. The necklace chimed — not sound, exactly, but a sensation. Down in the vein, the faint light answered.

"This was a crossing," he said. "A place where flows met and people tried to say, Here the world may change and not break."

"Did it work?" Genn asked.

"It worked long enough to be remembered," Derwin said. "That's something."

They explored quietly out of respect. Lira found a coil of dried vine tucked into a crack in one standing post — a bracelet made for a wrist far smaller than any here. Genn uncovered a shard of smooth black glass and held it up, squinting. "Obsidian?" he asked. Derwin shook his head. "Ash made hard," he said.

“Pressed until it forgot to flow.” He ran a thumb along the shard’s edge. It had been a blade once. Maybe something else afterward.

Bramble stood at the ravine’s mouth like a statue, but every muscle shouted readiness. Twice he flicked an ear toward the west, then went still again. Derwin trusted that more than any rune. Whatever hunted them was farther than a run but closer than a day.

Along the far wall of the ravine, half-hidden by a fall of roots, Lira found marks that were not petroglyphs. She called Derwin over, and together they pried back the roots and scrubbed at the rock with wet moss until the marks resolved into letters cut deep, angry. The script was druidic — of an age when people wanted to leave words very badly indeed.

WE HELD FOR THREE SEASONS.

WE FED IT LIGHT.

WE WOULD NOT FEED IT BLOOD.

Derwin traced the final line with a shaking finger. “They built against it,” he said, relief and grief cracking together in his voice. “And when it asked for what would bind most easily, they said no.”

Genn stared at the letters, jaw tight. “So what did do instead?”

Lira touched the first line: HELD. “Time,” she said. “They gave it time.”

Derwin let out a breath he hadn’t noticed he was holding. “And light,” he said, more softly. His hand wandered to the small stoppered vial in his pack — the drop of liquid light from the

Heart Tree's last dream. He did not take it out. Not yet.

They rested there — not long, but in a way that felt like the body's yes to the mind's no. Derwin drank from his flask and listened to the sighing of the veins. He tried to decide if the thrum under his skull felt weaker here or stronger, and he failed because the two felt like the same from different sides.

"Can we… fix it?" Genn asked, the way a boy asks knowing the answer will be a sermon.

"Not today," Derwin said. "But we can learn how it breaks."

They followed the ravine until it shallowed to a rocky spill and the ash veins dipped underground. Here the forest changed again — back to something that tried to look natural. Ferns unfurled, birds called in brief bursts like people clearing their throats, and a stream ran clear enough to count pebbles on the bottom. Derwin knelt and cupped water in his hands. It was cold and good. He let some spill on his wrists and throat until his pulse remembered something softer than flight.

When they rose, the day had edged toward afternoon, and the sun made what light it could. Bramble took the lead without being asked, and they let him; when the earth is confused, use the creature who still remembers it with his feet.

The path climbed through a stand of fir where the trunks had grown together in pairs, then to a ridge where the land, all at once, opened. They stopped without speaking.

Below them lay a valley of slow ruin. Rooflines stood where houses had been. A broken circle of stones marked where a communal hearth once burned. A field that had known grain for years wore only scrub. There was no smoke. The silence was not new; it was the kind that had time to settle into the wood.

Lira swallowed. “It’s… empty.”

Derwin listened. “Not empty,” he said. “Just done.”

They descended in a cautious zigzag, Bramble testing each switchback as if expecting the slope to shrug him off. At the first house — a low place of wattle and daub with a frame of bent saplings — Genn picked up a child’s play spindle from the dust and put it back exactly where he’d found it.

There were signs of hurried leaving: a chair tipped on its side; a half-baked loaf turned fossil in a cold oven; a rope with three knots in it fastened around a door-latch the way a grandmother might secure it against a night wind. But there were also offerings that looked like they’d been made after the leaving — small piles of smooth stones under windows, black ribbons tied around the ends of beams, driftwood carved into tiny boats and left in doorways as if to wish the house a safe crossing.

Derwin breathed in slowly through his nose and let the air sit behind his eyes. “They came back to mourn,” he said. “But not to stay.”

At the center of the village stood a green that had forgotten it was a green. The grass was calf-high, and seedheads bowed as they do when no one bothers to cut a path. In its middle, a young oak had found a way. Its trunk wore a wreath of carved tokens, each no bigger than a palm, strung on twine that had been replaced more than once. Names cut into wood, smoothed by hand. Some shallow, some deep. Each a held breath.

Lira’s fingers hovered over the wreath. “Do we read them?”

Derwin shook his head. “We remember them without learning them. Some names are not for us.” He knelt and touched two fingers to the soil at the oak’s base. The ground felt… willing.

Tired, but willing.

A sound like a footstep whispered behind them. Bramble turned first; Derwin followed, hand on staff. A figure stood at the edge of the green — a woman in a faded cloak, hood back, hair threaded with ash. She did not reach for a weapon. She kept both hands open and at her sides.

"Who are you?" Genn asked, more bold than wise.

The woman glanced at the wreath and then at Derwin. "The one who kept the names," she said. Her voice was raw but not brittle. "Until others could carry them."

Lira took a step forward, then stopped, checked by a look from Derwin. A plea for gentleness.

"We don't take," Derwin said. "We came to listen."

The woman nodded as if she hoped he would say something like that and had prepared herself not to be disappointed. "Then listen with your feet," she said. "Walk where they walked last." She pointed toward a path that led out of the far side of the green into low brush and the suggestion of a stream.

They followed. The woman did not come with them. She returned to the oak and the names.

The path led to a short rise and then to what had once been a footbridge over a creek. The bridge was gone, burned or taken, but the creek had narrowed so much from drought or wound that they could step across. On the far bank, the ground was darker, as if the soil had been soaked and dried and soaked again. Ash had been raked into furrows and then scattered and then raked again by hands that wanted desperately for the ground to forgive them.

A ring of stones marked a place where people had stood and said words that hurt. Derwin could feel the ache in his knees even before he knelt.

He touched the central stone and felt the same faint thrum he'd felt at the crossing of veins, only thinner, more human. Not old work. New. Desperate.

"We said them here." The woman appeared behind them. They hadn't heard her approach. "We sent the names on and begged the ground to keep the steps that were left."

Lira's eyes were bright. "Did it?"

"For a time," the woman said. "Until the lines began to hum again." She looked past Derwin, toward the hills. "They are humming now."

Derwin stood and bowed his head to the place. He reached into his pack and touched the vial again.

"Will you teach us your rite?" he asked.

The woman looked at his hands. She nodded once. "If you will teach us how to make it more than farewell."

They returned to the green at sunset. The woman lit a small fire of dry herb and thin wood; the smoke smelled like rain that couldn't quite remember where it used to fall. She set a bowl at the foot of the oak, poured clear water into it, and said a greeting not to the tree but to the space the tree kept.

Derwin waited until she was done. Then he asked for a wisp of Bramble's fur and burned it in the same smoke. He took a pinch of clean soil from his pouch — earth he had carried from the old grove before he'd ever let himself admit why — and let it fall into the bowl where it clouded and then cleared. He did not pour it on the roots. He did not ask for anything.

The woman knelt opposite him. From beneath her cloak

she drew a shard of ash-veined stone, edges polished by long handling. She pressed it flat to the ground. "This place remembers the bright touch," she said. "Not the sun's, not fire's. A light the earth has never seen again. Ash veins hold its echo. But only those who carry enough of their own may draw from it."

Derwin's chest tightened. "How?"

She gestured to the bowl. "You call the vein close by gesture, not by strength. With earth, with breath, with a thing that lives still. Then you wait to see if the ground agrees."

Her fingers traced a simple spiral on the stone, then pressed her palm flat. The soil beneath her hand quivered. Slowly, a bead of brightness welled up through the crack like dew forming where no dew belonged. She touched the bead to the bowl's water; it sank and shimmered like a second sky.

Derwin stared. "It's… alive."

"No," she said. "It is remembering. That is all."

She pushed the stone toward him. His hands shook as he mirrored her motion: spiral, breath, palm flat. For long moments nothing answered. Then, faintly, a flicker — as if the ground hesitated, weighing him. He closed his eyes and let himself breathe for the grove that was gone, for the children at his side, for the stubborn beast who had carried him this far. The soil loosened. A droplet of liquid light rose and trembled on his palm.

He guided it into the water bowl. The surface flared once, then steadied, glowing from within.

“Most can only call one drop,” the woman said. “Some none. Fewer still can shape it to last.” From a pouch at her belt she drew a thin glass vial and offered it to him. “Seal it while the memory is fresh. It will fade if you linger.”

Derwin uncorked the vial and, with a steadiness that surprised him, coaxed the droplet into it. The glass cooled sharply as the light settled inside, pulsing faint but sure. He stoppered it tight and pressed the vial to his chest.

“We held for three seasons,” he said, echoing the words carved in the ravine. “We fed it light. We will not feed it blood.”

Lira, watching with eyes wide and wet, let her small glow leak from her fingers into the bowl. The water did not blaze. It remembered. That was enough.

Genn stood with his fists at his sides, hating how clumsy he felt. Then, after a long hesitation, he took the spindle from the abandoned house and set it beside the bowl. He said nothing. The gesture was the light he had to give.

When the rite was done, the woman took a token from the wreath and pressed it into Derwin’s palm. There was no name cut into it. The wood was blank and smooth.

“For the ones who are not lost yet,” she said. “So you remember to keep a place for them.”

Derwin closed his fingers around the token like it might fly. In his other hand, the vial of light cooled but did not dim. He knew, without needing to be told, that he would one day need it — and that another drop might yet be called again.

The woman returned to the oak and the not-empty village and

did not look back.

Night came down in layers. They made a small camp on the ridge above the valley where the wind and stars could find them. Bramble lay so that his body made a wall on the side the children slept. Lira watched the bowl glow softly in her lap, the water no longer lit but no longer ordinary either. Genn turned the blank token over and over and over until the motion soothed whatever part of him had learned to count threats.

Derwin lay on his back and listened to the ash veins hum under everything: the old crossings, the new lines, the places where people had held and refused and held again. He thought of the crow's voice and of the woman's hands and of the stubborn light flickering under the tar.

"Not from here," the old voices had said. "Not from now."

Then we teach it, he thought, as if teaching were a verb that could hold a world.

He did not sleep long. In the hours when the night is thinnest, when loss makes its most convincing arguments, he dreamed of an oak that grew out of a bowl of water and of a child's hand pressed flat to the bark. When he woke, the bowl in Lira's lap was dark again, but the token in Genn's hand felt warm.

At first light they rose. The forest stretched itself and pretended it was simply a forest. Bramble shook out his mane and tested the air and looked to Derwin for the nod he was already giving.

They did not go back to the ravine of the crossing. They went forward, following the ground's oldest advice: step where it holds, and do not be the first to break what's bearing you. The ash veins kept humming, the way a wound hums when it decides to heal or not and is letting you know which.

By midmorning a faint column of smoke rose on the far horizon, thin as a finger, no broader than a promise. Derwin shaded his eyes and did a careful math he didn't teach to children.

"Another village?" Genn asked.

"Or what's left of one," Derwin said.

They looked at each other the way people do when they're about to write their names in a book they have never read and cannot put down. Then they went, the ridge rolling out like a spine under their feet, Bramble's breath in time with the morning's, the old crossings under them like a map made by someone who loved them and someone who did not.

Chapter Eighteen

They reached the smoke by midday, and it was the good kind—gray and thin, marked by wet wood and herb, not the oily pitch that chased people from their own doors. The trail descended into a shallow dell where a creek ran slate-blue over stones, and where a handful of tents had been raised close together the way frightened animals fold in against a storm. Children's clothing hung on lines between alder branches. A stew-pot simmered over a low fire. There was laughter here, but the kind that looks over its shoulder first.

Bramble stopped at the edge of the clearing. He breathed once, long and slow, and Derwin felt the sound in his ribs. Genn and Lira held back until he stepped forward.

A woman from the camp rose to meet them. She had the posture of someone who remembered how to stand before she remembered why. A string of wooden tokens circled her throat like a second spine.

"We saw you from the ridge," she said. "And the beast. Either you're lost or you're looking for trouble."

"Both, lately," Derwin answered. He kept his hands open and away from the dagger. "We're not here to take or ask. We came because of the smoke."

The woman's eyes flicked to Genn and Lira, then back to Bramble. "Keep your fires low," she said, softer now. "The wind tells on us."

"We will. I'm Derwin."

"Vaela," she replied, "of Irn Hollow. What's left of it."

Derwin nodded toward the tokens at her throat. "You keep the names."

"I keep the remembering," Vaela said. "Names are only tools if the hands are willing."

She led them through the tents. There were perhaps thirty souls here, most older or very young, with only a scattering of the in-between. The in-between moved like hinges—fetching water, mending boots, stirring the stew no one was hungry for and everyone needed. At the creek's bend stood a frame of willow boughs tied with black ribbon, and hanging from it a lattice of carved tokens, each the size of a palm, each strung on its own loop of cord.

Lira touched one with the back of her knuckle and pulled her hand away quick, as if afraid the wood would whisper back.

"Do you add to them every day?" Derwin asked.

"Only on the days that forget we are still living," she said. "We don't add the lost lightly. The children carve the letters. Their hands shake and the lines wander, and that is how we know we are not done."

Vaela led them to the willow frame. "We are carving more." She swept aside a cloth to reveal a low table with a dozen blanks, a knife, and a half-charred stick of pigment used to darken the grooves of letters so they could be read at a distance. It looked like the stump of a thorn.

Derwin took in the table, the tokens, the creek. "Will you let me help?"

"Help or lead?" Vaela asked.

"Help," he said. "And beg to learn."

They waited until the light turned old-gold on the alders. Then the camp gathered by the frame—no drums, no chant, just a shifting of feet and the friction of people arranging themselves into a shape that could bear weight. Vaela stood at the water's edge and lifted one hand. Silence came because the people willed it.

"We set the names in the bright," Vaela said. "So the night cannot pretend it owns them." She nodded to Derwin.

Derwin knelt at the creek, palms resting on his thighs, and let the field of attention settle. He didn't reach for a spell. He reached for listening—down through his breath into the rocks and then into the slower current beneath it all. The forest did not hide its ache here; it trembled like someone holding back a sob so they could say what had to be said first.

Bramble lowered his head to the creek and drank, the water braiding around his muzzle and riffled fur. When he lifted it, a few of the youngest children dared come closer, then closer still, until one bold boy pressed a palm to Bramble's shoulder and said, "Thank you," without looking at Derwin at all.

"Why do you thank him?" Lira asked gently.

"Because the fear is quieter when he breathes."

Genn and Lira knelt beside him. Lira's hands glowed faintly, a quiet lumen that came and went with her breath. Genn fidgeted and then stilled, jaw stubborn, eyes wet.

Vaela lifted the first token. "Rion of Irn Hollow," she said. "Who ran the grain-house. Who told bad jokes to make the floorboards laugh." She handed the token to Derwin.

Derwin cupped it between both hands. He did not picture a face. He pictured a floorboard and the way a body might stand above it to make it creak on purpose. He set the token against the water until the ripples washed through its grain, then placed it on the willow lattice where the sun could find it at least once a day when there was sun to find.

The next token. "Sere, daughter of Maeth," Vaela said. "Who carried water in both hands and dust on her mind. Who could not bear that her feet were small." A girl no older than Lira brought the token forward, her fingers shaking, and Lira steadied her wrist without stealing the work from her.

"Speak with the wood," Derwin murmured. "It remembers trees. Trees remember long."

They set a dozen names. Then a dozen more. Some the camp spoke out loud, and some they only breathed through their teeth, a sound like rope drawing tight across a post. A man with a broken nose brought a token without letters, only a deep gouge through the center.

"Whose?" Vaela asked.

"The boy who did not come back," he said. "I could not… I could not ask the knife to say it."

Derwin took the token and held it to his chest. He felt the old ache rise, the one made of each small promise he had failed to keep and every large one that kept him. He pressed the token to the water and whispered the only true thing he had for a stranger. "Be carried."

When the last token was hung, the camp did not disperse. They waited.

Vaela turned to Derwin. "We have only ever sent them on," she said. "Is there a way to make the ground remember differently?"

Derwin swallowed. He thought of the ravine, the carved words, the stubborn light flickering under tar. He thought of the drop of liquid light wrapped in cloth in the deepest pocket of his pack.

Not yet, he told himself again.

"There is a way to teach the place to hold," he said. "It is not grand and not quick." He stood and beckoned Genn and Lira. "It starts with tending what the night can still love."

They walked the edge of the creek together. Derwin showed them how to lay small stones so the water spoke a little louder over them; how to tie a ribbon of clean cloth to the alder so the wind would learn a softer sound; how to bury a pinch of honest soil where no one would see and everyone would feel it when they crossed.

Genn scoffed—softly. "This is… nothing."

"It is a lot of nothings," Derwin said. "Which is how a forest remembers to be itself." He put Genn's hand on the bark. "Your stubbornness is good. Teach it to work on what can be kept."

They returned to the lattice. The children were calmer now, the kind of quiet that comes after work that doesn't have to be explained. Bramble lay beside the creek with his eyes half-closed. His ear flicked at every sudden sound, then settled when it was only wind and pot-lids.

Vaela untied the tokens at her throat and placed them one by one on the low table. "I have kept them long enough," she said. "Let the others carry." The camp murmured—not grief, but a sound like relief's older cousin saying, *at last*.

As dusk drew down, Derwin spoke to the camp. He did not make a speech. He only told them what he knew of the ash veins and of the old hands that had refused to feed them blood. He taught the simplest cleansing—breath, water, watching—and left out the parts that would tempt someone to try grandness before the ground trusted them. When he finished, no one thanked him, which is how he knew he had given them something true: they were busy using it.

They fed him and the children. Later, when the stars came out one at a time as if someone was counting, Derwin sat by the creek with Genn and Lira and listened to the not-silence of a camp making the night smaller.

“They asked us to carve,” Lira said. Her hands still smelled of resin and smoke. “It felt… like carrying and being carried.”

Genn turned the blank token—Vaela’s counterpart to the one from the valley—over and over in his palm. “There was one boy,” he said. “He didn’t put a name up. He asked me if there was a way to keep a space instead. For a brother who might come back.”

“What did you tell him?” Derwin asked.

“I said I didn’t know. And then I showed him how to tie a ribbon so the wind would know a softer sound.” He looked embarrassed. “It felt like lying.”

“It was the best kind of truth,” Derwin said. “The kind that can be kept without breaking.” He stared at the water until the world became only ripples. “Sometimes the names you don’t speak are the ones that keep you standing when the ones you do speak try to throw you down.”

They rested with the camp that night. Bramble took the

outermost circle, laying his bulk along the path the wind liked best. Twice he rose and went a little way into the dark, and twice he came back with dew on his muzzle and a patience in his shoulders that made the children's breathing even out.

Before dawn, someone began to hum. It started near the stew-pot and wandered through the tents, picked up by whoever needed a small rope to hold. Lira woke to the sound and didn't try to sleep again. She sat up and watched the first light frost the willow frame and the wooden names. Every token shone a little, as if the night had tried to wear them and given them back just before morning.

Vaela found Derwin by the creek and offered him a small bundle wrapped in dyed cloth the color of alder-catkins. Inside lay three blanks and a slender, well-used carving knife.

"You'll find more," she said. "It is not a gift anyone wants. But you will be angry if you have to ask for it later."

Derwin nodded. He did not say he already had two blanks in his pack. He didn't have to.

"Where will you go?" he asked.

"North," Vaela answered. "There is a stand of beeches that remembers how to be a roof. We will try again to make a village where the rain does not feel like a stranger." She glanced at Genn and Lira, who were helping a boy tie his ribbon to the alder. "You will keep the children close?"

"As close as the work lets me," Derwin said. "And closer when it doesn't."

Vaela's mouth softened. "Then take this as well." She lifted the last token from her throat—a small oval, blank on both sides, the grain fine and straight. “For the name you cannot imagine yet.”

When they took their leave, the camp did not gather to see them off. It kept doing. It kept remembering. Derwin found he preferred it that way. Bramble stepped back onto the trail with a low huff and shook creek water from his fur as if shaking off someone else’s grief.

They climbed into the day. The trees stood closer together, and the ash smell thinned with altitude, replaced by the peppery green of crushed fern and the copper note of wet stone. Genn asked questions until he ran out of breath; Lira answered half of them with guesses that made Derwin want to be right for her.

An hour past midday, they reached a shelf of rock where the world flipped open again and presented them the far hills, blue as the inside of a mussel shell. Beneath it, stitched into the patchwork of slope and creek and stand of alder, another thin finger of smoke rose.

“More survivors?” Lira asked.

“Or more remembering,” Derwin touched the new blanks in his pack. He touched the vial he still would not use. He touched the token he still could not name. “Either way,” he said, “we keep walking.”

Bramble snorted once in agreement and took the lead. The wind came up the valley with a sound like ribbon on bark. For a moment, the names on the willow frame all gleamed at once. Then the light shifted, and the forest pretended it had not been watching at all.

Chapter Nineteen

The day broke pewter-gray and thin, the kind of light that made every surface look a little tired. They left Vaela's dell behind with the creek's hush still in their ears and the soft weight of new blanks in Derwin's pack. Far ahead, the thread of smoke they'd marked the day before unspooled into a smear; closer at hand, the forest breathed in shallow pulses as if bracing for a blow it already knew was coming.

Bramble took the lead. Where the trail narrowed to a knife, he went slow. Where the brambles thickened—his brambles—he nudged the others toward the low places where the land remembered how to be gentle. Twice he stopped dead and turned one ear; twice Derwin waited, listened, and chose a different path without asking why. Genn and Lira walked close, the kind of close that pretends to be casual and isn't.

They found the wardens by accident—or perhaps the wardens allowed themselves to be found. A whistle, low and two-noted, curled out from a stand of alder. Three figures rose from the understory, all mud-smeared and bark-camouflaged: two young, one gray at the temples with eyes like flint in rain.

"Hold," the gray one said, palm lifted. Then, seeing Bramble, he amended, "Hold and be grateful the forest sometimes loans us miracles."

Derwin lowered his staff. "We're not your enemy."

"If you were," the gray man said, "you wouldn't be speaking to me yet." He looked Derwin over. Noted the patched robe, the cracked staff, the children, the beast. "Name?"

"Derwin."

That got a longer look. A flicker of a name remembered poorly and a rumor remembered well. "Sitha," the man said at last. "Warden of Reedglass Fen. Or what's left of it. You've walked the ash veins; I can smell them on you. You've come at the right time and the wrong place."

"The fen?" Derwin asked.

"Turns against us even while we stand on it," Sitha said. "The crow's hands seeded it with things that rot as they grow. We try to push in. The ground fights back." He jerked his chin at Derwin's companions. "They yours?"

"They are themselves," Derwin said. "But yes."

Sitha stared another heartbeat, then nodded once. "Come see it. If you run, run uphill."

Reedglass Fen

The fen announced itself by smell first: the mineral-sour reek of peat turned inside out, the copper-sweet of old blood leeched into water, the cold musk of rot that hadn't decided yet if it would become soil or memory. Then came the sound—frogs in the reeds, yes, but off-beat, like a song interrupted too often. And then the sight.

The Reedglass was a wide silver sheet under the clouded sky, riddled with islands of reed and rush. Boardwalks stitched between them—lashed willow and alder planks, sunk stakes, the work of hands who understood that the land could be walked with and not just on. But the boardwalks sagged in places where the posts had blackened, and old paths had been rerouted into unhappy angles to avoid patches where the water went the wrong color.

Sitha led them across a narrow spine of planks that bowed under Bramble's weight. "Step where I step," he said without looking back. "And if it looks solid, assume it isn't."

They reached a dry hummock that held a scatter of warden gear: coil-ropes, oiled cloth, bundles of fire-hardened stakes, a clay map-stone scratched with crude marks. A dozen wardens crouched under a windbreak, faces turned to the fen. Two rose when Sitha approached; one kept his gaze on the water where a reed-bed made a slow circle as if pulled by a current no one else could see.

Sitha pointed with two fingers. "Yesterday we pushed to the old willow stand there." A far island with a ghost of a tree. "We set stakes and a simple ward-line. Night fell. The line held." His mouth thinned. "Before dawn the water under it went tar. Stakes turned to charcoal. The ward burned itself into silence."

"Mid-ward corruption," Derwin said, stomach tightening. "They're feeding it as you fight."

"Not just feeding," said a woman who hadn't taken her eyes off the water. "They're teaching it." She finally looked over—long braids, fierce mouth, a scar that forked over one eyebrow like a river map. "Nari," she said. "I keep the boardwalks alive. Or try." She jerked her chin toward the far reeds. "They're there. Not many. Enough. They sing to the fen like it's a dog they've starved. It comes when called."

Lira swallowed, watching the reed-bed complete another slow, wrong circle. "What do we do?"

"Break the song," Sitha said. "Or make it forget the words."

Derwin crouched at the map-stone. Someone had pressed

symbols into the clay with a stick: circles for islands, lines for planks, X's where boardwalks had failed, a smear where someone's hand had dragged in anger.

"Let me hear it," Derwin said.

Sitha didn't ask what he meant. He gestured to Nari, who lifted a hand. The boardwalk team went still. Even the frogs seemed to listen.

At first, there was only wind and water. Then, at the edge of hearing, a thread—too regular for nature, too thin for comfort. It wove through the reeds, a melody built on wrong intervals that made Derwin's teeth ache. Under it, a second sound: the slow thump of something like a heartbeat, but arrhythmic, as if it refused to sync with anything that lived.

"That," Derwin said softly, "is not the fen's voice."

"No," Sitha said. "But the fen remembers hunger. They use that."

Derwin's hand slipped to the willow-and-copper necklace at his throat. He felt the cool of the moon-charms and a tremor he couldn't name. He thought of the dagger his parents had left—the blade that took on the color of the wielder's intent. He did not draw it. Not yet. He walked to the water's edge and crouched until the marsh's breath dampened his face.

"The land wants to be asked," he murmured. "Not commanded." He glanced back to Genn and Lira. "If I tell you run, run to Nari. If I say pull, pull the rope. If I fall—"

"You won't," Lira said, and said it as if the world owed her that much truth. Genn didn't speak. He tied the new carving knife to his belt.

Derwin stepped out onto the boardwalk.

The First Push

They went as a knot: Sitha with a spear, Nari with a coil of rope and a mallet, two wardens with stakes, Derwin with his staff, Genn and Lira behind him, Bramble last—massive, sure-footed, silent as a boatswain that knows the river better than its captain. The reed-beds parted and closed with a hiss. Twice something bumped the underside of the planks; once the whole line swayed when water boiled black against a piling.

They reached the old willow hummock. The "willow" was three split trunks fused by moss and memory. Ten paces beyond, an island of sedge shivered and a shape lifted from it—a figure in tattered gray, antlers woven into his hood, hands black to the wrist.

"Back," Nari hissed. "He sees us."

Derwin raised his palm. "No. Let him see." Then he lifted his voice. "I know your song."

The figure's head tilted. When he spoke, the sound came like breath blown over a bottle's mouth. "You have forgotten more than you remember. Lay down your stick, green man. The marsh will carry you gentler than your friends will."

"I keep the living," Derwin said. "You harvest the dying."

"Harvest?" The hooded head cocked again. "No. We accelerate. Rot is only memory sped up." He spread his hands. The reeds around him shuddered and blackened, then sprang back greener than before. "See? We make time honest."

Behind the figure, two more rose—one to either side—staves

sunk into the muck, mouths moving. The thin song tightened. The boardwalk trembled underfoot.

"Stakes," Nari snapped. The warden with the mallet drove a new one through the planks into the peat. Derwin set his staff against it and whispered. The stake answered and refused to move. The boardwalk steadied.

The antlered figure watched with interest. "You ask. How quaint." He plunged a hand into the water and lifted it dripping with tar. "We tell." He flicked the blackness. It hit the planks and crawled toward them like a living oil.

"Lira," Derwin said calmly, "strings of light around the oil only. Don't fight it—frame it."

She raised both hands. A filament shimmered out from her fingers like spider-silk at dawn, sketching a delicate loop around the creeping tar. Where the light touched, the sludge hesitated, as if uncertain whether it had reached a shore.

"Genn," Derwin said, "stakes in a triangle—here, here, and here." He tapped with his staff. "Tie them with the rope you made for Vaela's alder. The rope remembers what you asked of it."

Genn's mouth opened to argue, then closed. He hammered the first stake like he wanted to split the fen in half. The rope—clean cloth twisted with reed—went taut between the stakes and hummed a note that did not belong to the marsh.

Derwin put his palm to the planks. "Not a wall," he whispered to the fen. "A pause."

The boardwalk stopped trembling. The tar-limb oozed up to the light-thread and touched it, making a sound like someone sucking their teeth. It didn't cross.

The hooded figure lowered his hand. "Clever," he said, and it was not mockery. He took one step sideways along his sedge-island; the island moved with him. "But you cannot hold a river with ribbon." He bent a glance at Lira. "That one learns quickly. Send her to me when you tire. The crow has a gift for children."

Bramble rumbled. The sound rolled out over the water and came back thinner, but it carried teeth.

Derwin raised his staff. "Nari," he said, "I need a clear run to that island. We can't win it, but we can make it remember us."

Nari flashed him a grin like a blade. "On my word—
jump." She signaled with three quick hand-cuts. The wardens along their line pulled ropes; planks shifted; a narrow bridge presented itself where moments ago there had been a gap wide enough to swallow a horse. "Now," Nari barked.

Derwin ran.

Mid-Field

The sedge bowed under his weight and then held—no argument, only surprise. The antlered figure drifted backward like a leaf on oil. Derwin leapt to another hummock, drove his staff into its edge, and sent a plea into the peat, "Let them slip. Let us stand."

For one heartbeat, the fen agreed.

Two black-robed chanters stumbled. Their staves struck the muck and stuck. Derwin lunged and swept his staff low; one staff went skittering into open water and sank like a thought that didn't want to be remembered.

The antlered figure hissed, and the fen changed its mind.

Water surged up through the sedge as if some invisible hand had squeezed the whole marsh. Derwin's feet slid. He went to one knee. The antlered figure reached with his voice and the thin song became a rope.

It lashed Derwin around the chest.

He could have cut it with light. He could have tried. Instead, he inhaled and did the one thing the song did not expect—he leaned into it. He let the rope pull him two steps forward and then stumbled sideways, giving it nothing to grip. The song faltered, the rope slackened, and he tore free with skin burned raw where sound touched flesh.

A cry from the boardwalk—Lira. "Derwin!"

He didn't turn. "Hold the frame," he called back, "no matter what I do."

The antlered figure lifted both hands now, and the water between them seethed. Something pale rose and broke the surface—a spine, then ribs, then a skull that had never belonged to any deer Derwin had known. The bones knit as he watched, clothed themselves in something like flesh and unlike it, a body taught the wrong book of how to be alive.

Derwin's stomach went cold. "No," he said, and wasn't sure whether he spoke to the man or the marsh. "You don't want this."

The thing took its first breath with a wet flute's rattle.

"Bramble!" Derwin shouted.

The beast was already moving. Planks clattered under his weight; ropes sang; wardens swore and leapt aside. Bramble hit the sedge like a landslide and met the thing with antlers. Bone cracked. The thing lurched back. Bramble stamped, stamped again, each strike a sentence: No. No.

The antlered figure stepped aside, almost lazily. "You could be useful," he called to Bramble. "You aren't made like the others. You don't listen to the same rules. Your hunger could learn ours."

Bramble's only answer was to rip one of the thing's forelimbs free with his teeth and fling it into the fen.

Derwin drove his staff into the muck and called a small, bright thing, the memory of spring. It rose in a dome that touched Bramble's shoulder and his own chest and made the reeds shiver as if a warm wind had gone through them. Where it sat over the thing, the flesh smoked and the bones showed.

"Enough," the antlered figure said, impatience at last. He cut his hand downward. The sedge under Derwin gave way.

He dropped like a stone into the fen.

Under

Cold slammed his chest and wrapped him in old leaves. His mouth filled with the taste of last-year's rain and the iron ghost of things that had bled here and been forgotten badly. He did not fight upward. He went still and listened.

The blight moved differently underwater. It wasn't a stain here—it was a grain, a silt that swirled among the clay. When it touched him, it recoiled like a dog singed by a cooking fire. The immunity he had half-known, half-feared, spoke in the water as simply as hunger or thirst: *This does not cling.*

He opened his eyes.

Light was thin. Reeds braided themselves into green bars around a murkier distance. In that distance, three shapes hung in the water—totems shoved into the peat like spears. Even without breath, he could feel them singing.

He kicked once, twice, and recognized the angle of the boardwalk above, the place where Lira's filament glowed faintly like a dawn that had missed the appointment. He swam deeper instead of higher and reached the first totem.

It looked like a root carved into a mouth. He put his hand over that mouth and pressed. The totem shook. He remembered Kesa's voice: *Not all things welcome a soft unmaking. Say the name of their purpose and give them a better one.*

Derwin mouthed the words into the water. "You called hunger. Call rest."

He pushed. The totem slid. The song frayed.

Above him, the boardwalk shook with a new impact. He felt Bramble's weight move and knew the beast had planted himself over the hole in the fen. Derwin went to the second totem, closer to the antlered man now—so close he could see, through water and sedge and shadow, the outline of that woven hood.

"Your boy drowns," the hooded figure called. "Let him. The marsh would have him gentle."

"Derwin!" Lira yelled again. A sob under his name.
He put his palm to the second totem's mouth. "You learned obey. Learn endure." He wrenched it sideways and, when it

refused to budge, drew the dagger.

The blade didn't shine under water. It darkened, taking on the color of the fen the way it took on the color of Derwin's intent. And his intent wasn't light now—it was stubbornness, the same that had kept a boy upright when every adult in a circle considered the ash a better fate. He cut. The totem split like old wood under a seasoned axe.

The song loosened.

The third totem sang louder in response.

He kicked for it. Something moved in the corner of his eye—a pale limb groping—then stopped, as if the water itself had gently laid a hand over it and said: *Later*.

He reached the third mouth and felt the carver's marks under his fingertips. The work wasn't old—this was a fresh wound. A signature repeated itself on the bevel, a mark like a bird's footprint. The crow's mark.

He set the flat of the dagger against the mark and thought of Vaela's frame and the names it held against the night. "Hold this instead," he told the totem. "Hold the ones who will not go under." He drove the blade down and split the mark through.

The song broke.

He kicked for the surface and came up under Bramble's chest.

Break and Flood

Hands grabbed his arms. The world hauled him out. He coughed up a fen's worth of old weather and the last of the thin song. Lira's hands were on his face and his shoulder and his mouth trying to decide which mattered most. Genn swore at him in a whisper so fast it turned into one word.

Across the water, the antlered figure stood very still. If disappointment had a posture, it was his. “You take and take,” he said. “And you call that healing.”

Derwin’s teeth chattered. “We take poison out of a wound,” he said. “Then we teach the skin to be skin again.” He forced himself to his feet. “Nari—your berm. Can we break it without drowning everything that isn’t trying to kill us?”

“The north berm?” She spat into the fen. “If we open it, the old channel runs. The nests go. The frog chorus resets from the beginning.” She met his eyes. “If we don’t, the song will return here by night.”

He looked from Lira to Genn to Bramble. The beast leaned against him, soaking and breathing hard, a warm mountain pretending it wasn’t tired.

Derwin listened to the frogs. Their calls came off-time and wrong, but alive.

He closed his eyes. The map of the fen rose. He saw where the water wanted to go and where people asked it politely to detour. He saw the place where the berm did not remember being old.

“Not the north,” he said. “Here.” He pointed to a hummock forty paces to their right—low, grass-topped, drained by three cut ditches. “If we open this, the water goes back to the cut creek-bed. We lose nests,” he said, and the words tasted like apology. “But we keep the alder stand and most of the reed-labyrinth. We buy time.”

“Or we make them angry,” Sitha said.

"They're already angry. This way we're honest about it."

Nari's grin returned. "I like honest." She looped rope around a stake and tossed the loose end to Genn. "On my count."

They ran the line of rope across the planks. Two wardens shouldered a log like a battering ram. Derwin set his staff into the peat at the berm's narrowest point and whispered again, and again—small words, hard ones, and the kind that ask rather than command. "Loosen. Remember fall. Let go the thing that is not yours to hold."

"Now," Nari said.

The ram struck. The peat bucked. Water, that had been holding its breath for years and then months and then days, chose a direction and remembered how to move. It punched through the weak place and took the path Derwin pictured.

The fen's song changed.

The thin wrong melody stuttered. The heartbeat under it tripped and missed and couldn't find itself again. Water raced along the re-opened channel and undercut the sedge where the antlered figure stood.

For the first time, he looked surprised.

He took a step back—and misjudged. The sedge gave under him. He fell to one knee, hands flung out. The island caught him and did not like it.

"Bramble," Derwin said, too soft for anyone else. The beast understood. He launched. The island lurched. The antlered figure rolled clear and slid to a second patch that held.

He lifted his head and smiled the way a man smiles when he decides he doesn't like a game enough to play fair. "Enough lesson," he said. "Now punishment."

He plunged both hands into the fen up to his elbows and pulled up something that was not water, not mud. A skein of blackness, a loom's worth, a sheet.

He flung it.

Derwin had time to recognize the shape of its edge—the same bevel as the totem's mark—and knew he could not raise anything fast enough or large enough to catch it all.

Then Bramble stepped between him and the sheet.

The sound it made on fur was like hot fat on a griddle.

Bramble didn't howl out. He went very still. His eyes went very wide. The sheet hung on him, then began to sink in as if the beast himself were a fen for it to learn the map of.

"Lira!" Derwin shouted. "Light, all you have—don't burn him, burn the sheet!"

She threw her hands up and did not aim; she widened. The filaments that had been fine as silk became bands an arm's-width across, arcing between posts and reeds and Bramble's antlers. Where they touched the blackness it flinched and smoked and withdrew, not back toward the antlered man but inward, as if trying to hide in Bramble's chest.

Derwin slammed his palm to the beast's sternum. The blight under his hand recoiled from him as from fire. He pushed and refused to let it in. "This is mine," he told it, the way a mother tells a stranger the child in her arms is not theirs to take.

"This is mine."

The blackness fought him. It learned him. It hated him. It slid out of Bramble's chest in long, stringy strands and retreated across the light-bands until it reached open air. There it gathered itself and fell—no longer a sheet, only dirty rain.

Bramble's legs shook and he sank.

Derwin's head swam. His sight narrowed. He tasted iron again and realized he bit his own tongue bloody in the effort not to beg.

Across the water, the antlered figure bowed. "There is always a price," he said. "Pay soon." He took two steps back into the reeds and was gone, the sedge not so much opening as forgetting it had ever been there.

The skeletal thing lay in pieces. The song was broken. The channel ran brown-clear where the peat let it. Frogs did not sing right away. They waited the way people wait for a room to decide if it is safe to speak in again.

Nari blew out a breath. "Hate them," she said. "Hate them for making me choose between a frog and a child and a plank and a hundred-year-old alder and—all of it."

Sitha lifted his spear point and rested his forehead against the shaft. "We don't choose that," he said softly. "We choose where to stand when it all insists we must." He looked at Derwin. "You stood."

Derwin didn't answer. He had both hands buried in Bramble's fur. The beast's breath came fast and shallow, then deeper, then steadier. Lira kept the light up a moment longer than necessary, then let it go the way a singer lets go a note they loved.

"Genn," Derwin said hoarsely, "the vials Kesa gave. One only. Slowly."

Genn's fingers shook and then didn't. He uncorked the vial and poured a thin line along the track the sheet had left. Where the liquid touched, the fur lay flat again and the skin stopped trying to crawl away from itself.

Bramble blew a breath out like a bellows being set down at last.

Aftermath

They fell back to the warden hummock on legs that misremembered how their joints worked. Someone pressed a bowl of thick stew into Derwin's hands; someone else wrapped Bramble's chest with clean cloth dipped in willow tea. The beast endured it with a patience that made the youngest warden cry without noise.

"Casualties?" Sitha asked, already counting the faces and their shadows.

"Two wounded," Nari said. "No dead." Then, quieter, "None of ours."

Derwin set the bowl aside. "None of ours," he repeated, and heard the cowardice in it after the relief. "But this is only one mouth of the river. They'll open another."

"They already have," Sitha said, and pointed with his chin to a crow-standard lashed high in a stand of reeds farther west. Its cloth was black on black, marked with a symbol Derwin had seen carved into wood and bone: the bird's-foot splay.

"Orders," Nari said. "Sometimes they're careless with them when they think the ground is already decided."

Derwin and Genn took a skiff. Lira stayed with Bramble, though no one told her to. The skiff hissed over water that was honest again for now. At the standard, a leather satchel hung nailed to a half-sunk post. Derwin pried it free with the dagger's pommel. Inside: a sheaf of oiled paper and a thing like a map drawn by someone who did not believe maps should be legible to anyone but their friends.

Back on the hummock, they spread the papers under a weight of stones. The marks were columns of circles and lines, marked by moon-phases, locations named by symbols the crow liked: bone, beak, feather, eye. One column had a sigil Derwin now recognized—three bars crossed by two—overwritten three times until the ink soaked through. Under it, a word in common hand: TIDE.

"Tide of Blackroots," Genn read from a margin note, lips tight. "Push. Breach. Feast."

"Feast?" Lira said softly. "On what?"

"On us," Nari said.

There was a second paper: a letter spattered with fen water and something darker, its lines cramped, its grammar colder than the day. *To the Hand of Ash*, it began, *Your pupil learns quickly. She wants what we want though she calls it other names. Send me two more with spines. The reed wall will be soft by the new moon. The seed will take in the children first.*

Derwin read the line twice and then folded the paper like a wound you cover because you cannot yet bind it. He did not say Ashling's name. He didn't have to. Lira saw his face and set her hand on his sleeve.

Sitha looked out over the fen. "We bought a day," he said. "Two if they're called elsewhere." He inclined his head to Derwin. "We wouldn't have bought an hour without that flood."

"The frogs would disagree," Derwin said.

"Frogs never agree," Nari said. "They chorus. That's different."

They ate. They bound wounds with willow and honey. Genn slept for a moment and woke up panicked—then didn't apologize for it. Lira sang under her breath while she re-wrapped Bramble's chest, the same melody Vaela's camp hummed. Once, Bramble pressed his nose into her hair and breathed, and Lira shook like a string plucked hard, then went quiet again.

At dusk, Sitha lit a tiny fire—hands cupped close, no smoke, only enough flame to tell cold fingers they could be hands again. He set three small stones around it and said three names without tokens: two wardens who weren't in the count because they had no bodies to count with, and a third name Derwin didn't know. The fire took the names and held them warm and did not try to make sense of the rest.

When the stars came out in a grit of pinholes, Derwin took the satchel and papers a little way off and read them again. He traced the column of moon-phases and matched them, clumsily, to the calendar in his head. The new moon was soon. The "reed wall" in the letter could be Reedglass or any fen that still pretended it was more water than hunger. The seed will take in the children first.

He swallowed; it did not go down.

He wrote on the map-stone with a coal nub: a ring around the place where they opened the berm; a line to mark the old channel; three X's where the totems had been; a small crescent for the island that tried to hold the antlered man and, for a heartbeat, had succeeded.

Lira came and sat without speaking. She held her palms to the ember-light and looked at the papers upside-down.

"They mean to take the camp," she said. Not a question.

"Or the children from it," Derwin answered. "The letter wants me to know it knows what I fear."

"Then it's wrong," Lira said, and it wasn't bravado. "It doesn't know what we are."

Derwin smiled without meaning to. "What are we?"

She nudged his shoulder with her own. "Hard to drag."

Night Watch

They set a rolling watch. Sitha took the darkest hour, claiming his eyes already knew the worst they would see. Nari slept with her hand on the rope that tied the boardwalk to the hummock as if she were tethering a living thing. Genn slept with the carving knife under his palm. Bramble slept lightly and often woke not to stand but to lift his head and listen to something only he could hear.

Derwin sat with his back to Bramble and his knees pulled up, the willow-copper necklace cold against his collarbone. He held the dagger in his lap, still sheathed. He remembered the way it had taken the color of his refusal under water. He remembered the way the sheet tried to learn Bramble's shape from the inside. He remembered the letter's careful cruelty and the mark carved onto each totem.

He wanted to burn something. He wanted to plant something. He wanted to walk home. He wanted to lie down in the fen and let the old leaves make him into soil that would not be persuaded to feed a single wrong thing.

He did none of those. He pressed his palm to the boardwalk and listened for the fen's breath like a father listens for a fever to break. He heard it, eventually, settle into something closer to sleep and farther from mimicry.

When the eastern sky went from iron to pewter again, Sitha put a hand on his shoulder. "You bought us a dawn," he said. "Don't spend it all in one place."

Derwin stood, joints stiff and head full of white noise. He looked at Genn and Lira curled under Bramble's reach. He looked at the wardens' faces, made older by a single night in a place that thought it could teach time how to hurry. He looked at the papers again, and the sigil, and the word: TIDE.

"Two days," he said to Sitha. "Maybe three. Then this Tide breaks somewhere that hurts us worse."

Sitha nodded once. "We'll hold here until we're told to run. Reedglass won't teach them the wrong lessons easily."

Derwin put the satchel into his pack. He put the blank oval Vaela had given him next to it. He took a breath he did not quite have room for and said, "We go to the camp."

"That far?" Nari asked. "With the fen to cross and your beast walking less than he pretends?"

Derwin stroked Bramble's neck where the fur was scorched. "He'll carry me when I fall," he said. "Then I'll carry him when he does. Between us we'll be one whole fool walking."

Genn stretched and groaned. "Then we'd better start." He tried to sound older than he was and sounded exactly his age. Lira stood and tightened the strap on her satchel until it bit her shoulder and didn't complain.

Sitha offered Derwin his hand; they clasped wrists. "If you see the crow," the warden said, "tell him the fen spit in his cup and didn't apologize."

"I'd rather bring the cup back to you empty."

Nari walked them to the first bend in the boardwalk. "If the water lies, step on the shadows, not the light," she said. "If the ground sings, hum louder. If you must choose between two bad planks, choose the one that complains about it. Quiet wood breaks."

Derwin committed each to memory as if they were spells. Maybe they were.

They set out into a morning that didn't know which way to turn its face. The reed-labyrinth hissed and then stilled when Bramble moved. The reopened channel ran alongside them, brown and honest. Twice they passed places where the water had gone bright black and then faded again to a color that remembered how to be water. Once a heron watched them go by and decided not to have an opinion.

At the last hummock before the trees thickened and took the fen's place, Derwin stopped and looked back. The reed-beds looked like any reeds in a bad year. The wardens, small at their post, looked like any people doing a hard thing on a day that deserved better from the sky. The boardwalk cut a neat, improbable line. He pictured it holding. He pictured it failing. He pictured it rebuilt.

"Keep breathing," he said to the fen, and his breath came out in a cloud that made no promise at all.

Bramble nudged him forward.

They left the Reedglass behind.

What the Papers Meant

They climbed hard for an hour to shake the fen's water out of their clothes and bones. Under the trees the world remembered shadow the right way. Derwin let himself believe, for twenty breaths, that the sky might remember blue again.

Then they stopped to read the papers properly.

They spread them on a fallen trunk while Bramble stood guard and pretended he wasn't leaning on it. Lira went through the columns, marking likely dates with a charcoal nub. Genn translated the crow's symbols into the kind of words people spoke when they wanted to be understood by people who didn't love them yet. Derwin traced the map's nonsense and pulled shapes out of it the way one finds animals in clouds.

Three sites named by eye sigils formed a rough arc that pointed straight at the camp's valley. Two beak marks sat at either end of the arc as if to bite any help that tried to come from the east or west. The feather marks dotted the fenlands like breadcrumbs. The bone marks marched up the river that fed the camp's creek.

"They mean to move like a weather front," Derwin said. "Not a flock— a flood." He tapped the TIDE column. "This is how they time it. Not by day, by dark. By when we cannot ask help of the sun."

“Then we ask the moon,” Lira said, as if it were a person she would write a letter to.

Genn stabbed a finger at the camp’s valley. “We can get there by nightfall if we cut the switchbacks.” He looked to Bramble, a creature who could carry a boy and a man and a girl and a world if asked and who did not think much of the asking.

Derwin rolled the papers, wrapped them in oiled cloth, and tucked them deep. He touched the blank oval again. He did not want to know yet whose name it would carry. He did not want to grant the day that kind of prophecy.

He stood. “We run.”

They ran.

Bramble took the narrow deer-ways where the ground stayed springy. Derwin used the tether between them—the grip of knee, the hand at the withers, the breath that matched—until he could let his thoughts turn away into open ground and listen. Twice he felt the land stiffen beneath Brambles hooves and jerked his weight aside a heartbeat before the soil caved to reveal a root-ball full of ichor and black worms that writhed at the touch of air and then stilled, exposed and shy.

They passed a stand of beeches that had charred and then leafed again from the bottom, candles burned and reborn. The sight steadied him. He told himself to be a beech.

They crossed the ridge where he’d first seen the valley’s smoke days ago. No smoke now. Only a smear on the horizon that could have been rain.

“Please,” Lira said under her breath, and Derwin didn’t ask who she was talking to because he was the same kind of superstitious.

The trail dropped. The trees closed. The air cooled in a way that told him the creek was near and right and hadn't been taught any new songs yet.

At the last bend before the camp's outer path, Bramble halted so suddenly Genn grabbed mane and Derwin nearly bit his tongue again.

The beast lifted his head. He breathed and breathed again. He turned one ear. He whuffed.

Derwin felt it a heartbeat later—the land tightening like a muscle pressed by a cold hand. Not the crow. Not the ash veins. Something lighter and older, like moth-wings. A messenger.

He raised his palm.

A shimmer descended through the trees like a bit of fog that had lost its way. It drifted to his hand and pooled there, a thumb's-width of faint light. Not a wisp. Not quite a witchlight. Something the forest used when it wanted to be sure a child would not crush it by accident.

It pulsed. Once. Twice. Then it slid into his skin.

He saw—the space over the camp, and in that space a shadow traveling like weather, too far to say when, too deliberate to say if.

He opened his eyes to find that he had leaned into Bramble again the way he had underwater leaned into the song's rope until it forgot how to hold.

"What?" Genn demanded. "Is it—"

"Not yet," Derwin said. "But soon." He looked down at

his hand where the light had gone in. "And the forest is done speaking in riddles to people who came home too late."

Lira squared her shoulders. "Good," she said. "I prefer orders."

Derwin laughed, and it came out sounding like someone he wanted to be.

They took the last bend at a run.

They did not find a siege.

Not yet.

They found Mother Kesa on the path with two elders and five children carrying baskets of mint and lambs-ear and the kind of mushrooms that don't misbehave when you boil them twice. They found the outer guards alert and not afraid. They found the wind moving in the right direction.

Derwin dismounted before Bramble stopped and wrapped Kesa in his arms in a way that a year ago he would have apologized for and now did not. She made a surprised sound and then patted his back like he was either a boy or a man who had done the arithmetic correctly for once.

"You're early," she said into his shoulder. "Or the storm is late."

"Both," he said, voice rough. He held out the satchel and the wrapped papers. "We bought a day at Reedglass. We spent a day getting here. We have some left. Not much." He looked past her at the children, at the baskets, at Genn and Lira who were already telling two different versions of the same story to three children who understood that the truth is the parts that don't change when the teller does. "We have work."

Kesa's mouth softened and then tightened again. "We always do," she said. "Come. We will read what can be read and guess the rest. Then we will teach the wind to hum a little louder."

Derwin walked into the camp with the weight of a day bought and the shape of a night coming. Behind him, Bramble breathed as if he were not hurt at all, because he was home again for the first time since he had decided what that word meant.

The siege had not begun. The siege had already begun.

They moved.

CHAPTER TWENTY

The forest was not quiet that night. It breathed around Derwin, slow and strange, each gust of wind carrying whispers he could almost understand. Somewhere far off, a tree groaned as though straining under invisible weight. Bramble lay curled beside him, but even the great beast's sleep was uneasy—ears flicking at sounds no mortal ear should have caught.

Derwin drifted in and out of slumber, until the darkness beneath his eyelids gave way to light.

Not sunlight.

A pale, silver-gold luminescence, neither moon nor star, rippled through a vast expanse of trees. He stood in a forest that felt older than time, each trunk impossibly wide, roots curling like sleeping serpents across the soil. The air shimmered, fragrant with something halfway between blooming flowers and the scent of rain on ash.

Before him rose the Heart Tree.

It was whole again.

Every leaf glowed faintly, a thousand emerald lamps strung upon a lattice of living wood. The trunk pulsed with inner light, as if blood made of dawn itself ran beneath its bark. The ground at its base was covered in moss so soft it seemed to move, breathing in tandem with the tree. For a long moment, Derwin could do nothing but stare—the ache in his chest almost unbearable.

Then a voice.

"You're late."

Ashling stood on the far side of the Heart Tree, her hand resting lightly against its bark. She looked older than in his memories, but it was not time that had aged her—it was something sharper, like frost biting into green leaves. Her eyes, bright as ever, carried both hurt and something he could not name.

"Ashling," he said, but the sound of her name seemed to vanish before it could cross the clearing.

She tilted her head, studying him the way one studies a puzzle whose missing piece might yet be found. "You remember this place wrong. It never looked like this."

Derwin glanced around. The perfect symmetry of the branches, the way the light bent toward the tree—it did feel... curated. Idealized. "Then where are we?"

She smiled faintly, though there was no warmth in it. "Where you think you should have been. Where you wish you had stood, instead of turning away."

Her words cut sharper than any blade.

He stepped toward her, but the moss beneath his feet thickened, each step heavier, slower, as if the ground itself resisted him. "I didn't mean to leave you."

Ashling's hand lingered on the Heart Tree's bark. For a moment, she seemed to listen to it, her lips moving in silent response to some unheard language. Then she
looked back to him. "Intent doesn't undo what's been done. Roots grow where they're fed, Derwin. Even poison feeds something."

He opened his mouth to speak, but she raised a finger.

“You think you’ll heal this tree,” she said. “But what if it doesn’t want to be healed? What if the rot has made it stronger?”

The ground trembled, and the luminous moss darkened in streaks, veins of black running outward from the Heart Tree’s base. Derwin felt the shift in the air—the scent of flowers turning to the sharp tang of blight. His hand went instinctively to the dagger at his side, but when he looked down, it was no longer the same weapon. Its blade shimmered, half silver, half shadow, and he could not tell which edge would cut deeper.

Ashling watched him with that same unreadable expression. “You can plant seeds all you want. But the soil remembers.”

Somewhere, faintly, he heard a child’s laugh. It was familiar—achingly so—but distant, like memory carried on wind. Ashling heard it too, and her gaze softened just enough for him to see the shadow of the girl he had known.

“I don’t hate you, Derwin,” she said, almost gently.

He felt his breath catch.

“But I don’t forgive you, either.”

The moss rose higher around his legs now, almost to his knees, pulling him back. The light of the Heart Tree dimmed, replaced by a cold gleam that came from nowhere. Ashling stepped back, melting into shadow, her voice lingering like a final leaf clinging to a winter branch. “When you wake, remember this: not all roots want the same sun.”

The forest collapsed inward, the image of the Heart Tree shattering into splinters of light that cut and burned.

Derwin gasped, lurching upright in his bedroll, Bramble rumbling low beside him. His skin was damp with cold sweat, and the dagger at his side—the real one—gleamed faintly in the moonlight, as though it had overheard every word.

And for the first time since leaving the camp, Derwin wasn't sure if his path led toward saving Ashling... or if it led straight to losing her forever.

Chapter Twenty One

Dawn arrived on a hush and a bruise. The eastern sky wore a deep violet seam, and the settlement stirred like a creature nursing hidden wounds. Smoke from banked coals drifted low, hugging the ground as if reluctant to rise into a world that might soon burn again. Derwin woke to the sound of canvas laces shivering in the breeze and Bramble's slow, steady breathing—a metronome for a day that desperately needed rhythm.

He lay still and counted the beats.

One for the grove that was.

One for the camp that remained.

One for what would come.

Bramble lifted his head before Derwin did, ears pricking toward the treeline. All along the perimeter, watchfires guttered. The guards—older druids, younger foragers, anyone whose hands could steady a spear—shifted on their feet and stamped warmth into numb toes. It had rained toward midnight, the kind that slicked bark and filled footprints with silver. The world smelled washed and raw.

"Up," Derwin whispered to himself. Bramble rose with him, stretching in a ripple of earth-toned fur and stone-bone antlers, then bumping Derwin's shoulder in a gesture that had become a kind of morning benediction.

Outside, the camp's sounds overlapped into a functional music: kettle-lids clinking; low instructions from Joram near the eastern barrier; Kesa's soft, flinty voice by the healer's lean-to; the clack of wooden practice staves where Genn and Lira had already gathered the brave and the reckless to drill forms. Names were called; hands were checked; bandages unwound, replaced, tightened.

Derwin drank it in like tonic. It was not the grove—but it was a rhythm.

He started in the healer's space, because that had become the right place to begin. The tent smelled of nettle-steam and clean cloth. Kesa stood over a low table, grinding something dark into a paste with the heel of her palm. Her bracelets clicked softly as she worked, the metal dulled by years of smoke.

"You slept," she said without looking up.

"Mostly," he answered.

"Good. I'll need you steady." She nodded toward three cots. A boy with a swollen ankle, a woman with a deep cut in her arm where thorns had tried to keep her, and an older druid whose breath came too shallow to be comfortable. Kesa parceled tasks with the ease of rain beading on a leaf: warm the stones; bind the woman's arm; show the boy the ankle-breath—four counts in, four counts resting, four counts out—to coax swelling away. Derwin moved, hands remembering small mercies even when his mind churned elsewhere.

The older druid opened one eye and found him. "You again," he rasped. There was no malice in it. Only a dry surprise, as if the forest had set an old coin in his palm.

"Me again." Derwin tested ribs, listened to lungs, hummed the soft, low note that encouraged a chest to loosen. When Kesa returned with a kettle she watched him finish, then placed two small vials on the table—glassy, leaf-wrapped, the last of her stores.

"You'll take these when you go," she said.

"When…" not if. He didn't argue.

By midmorning the camp had woken fully. The ground along the northern approach was a choreography of work: saplings cut and bent into shallow arches; bark peeled, shaped, woven; cordage twisted from nettle and vine; stakes driven where the soil agreed to hold them. No wall would stop the blight, but a line might give a moment, and a moment might save a life.

Derwin set his staff across two rocks and lifted materials with Joram, shoulders burning. They moved without words at first. The silence was not friendship, but it was no longer war.

"Your form is worse than your teaching," Joram grunted finally, as Derwin misjudged the weight and had to correct mid-lift.

"Age," Derwin said.

"You're the same age as my patience."

"Then I am doomed."

Joram snorted, then jerked his chin toward the children practicing at the far end. "They listen to you."

"They humor me."

"They listen," Joram repeated. "That's rarer." His mouth pressed thin; he hadn't forgiven—Derwin didn't ask for it—but the ground between them was less thorn and more loam than it had been.

Genn and Lira had claimed the flattened earth near the old cooking ring. Ten children stood in two ranks, each with a shaved sapling or a practice staff, and Bramble watched from the shade with the enduring patience of a boulder. Lira barked counts; Genn corrected grips. When Derwin approached, the two exchanged a brief look—conspiracy and pride braided into it.

"Show me the spiral parry," Derwin said.

They tried. Half the line turned clean; the other half over-rotated and knotted themselves into each other's elbows. There was laughter, then embarrassment, then that brittle silence young bodies wear when they want to do well.

"Again," Derwin said, and he wove between them, tapping wrists, tilting chins. "Eyes up. Feel the weight travel. The staff is a river; you're not a dam; you're the shore." He took a place in the line and moved with them, slow the first time, then faster. By the fourth repetition the shape began to belong to them.

When they were breathing hard he set the staves aside and raised both hands. "Now the other work."

The Circle's breath. The tiny, elemental listening. He had taught this a hundred times before the world fell out from under him, and still it felt like learning how to walk every time he did it. "Root," he said quietly. "Breath. Notice."

They knelt. The ground was damp enough to stain their knees. At first there was only fidgeting, the itch of sweat and gnats. Then the edges softened. A breeze combed the grass. Somewhere under the surface, water moved. Even the camp's clatter diffused until it seemed to float above them.

"Some of you will hear nothing today," Derwin said. "That's not failure. It's patience. Some of you will want to force it. That's pride. Don't. If a door is closed, we don't kick it. We wait for the hinges to remember they were made to turn."

Lira's eyes were closed, jaw tight, the way she squeezed emotion until it yielded. Genn flinched when a fly found his ear, then grinned sheepishly and resettled. A small boy lifted his hands a fraction, as if a thought had touched him. Derwin felt the faintest shimmer under his own palm—like the last breath of a song.

He tried to deepen it. The shimmer withdrew. He smiled at the lesson and let it go.

Toward midday, the camp stilled of its own accord. A dozen villagers gathered near the east fire where a flat stone had been scrubbed clean. Each carried a sliver of wood, thumb-worry smooth. Some were etched with symbols; some were plain; all bore weight heavier than wood should carry.

Kesa stood beside the stone. Her voice, when it came, was not loud. It did not need to be. "We do not know all the names. But we speak them anyway. Silence is a kind of forgetting, and forgetting is a second death."

One by one they stepped forward. A woman with ash-streaked hair placed a token and said, "Bray." A man with bandaged fingers said, "Toma." A child, barely six, lifted two in both hands and whispered, "Rill and Rill," then clarified with grave precision, "the big one and the small one."

Derwin added nothing to the stone. He had long ago run out of safe places to set names. But when the murmuring faded, he reached into his pouch and touched the bracelet with the single carved letter— A. He did not place it on the stone. He did not yet deserve to. He pressed it into his palm until the corners bit skin and let the pain be a promise.

Kesa concluded with a low, thrumming chant that was more breath than sound. The air listened. Even the ravens quieted.

In the pale shade of afternoon, Derwin borrowed a child's charcoal stick and a scrap of stitched bark-paper. He'd written to Ashling before—half-letters that curled into ash on their own—but today the words came out of him like unspooled thread.

> Ashling,
>
> If the forest carried words, I would set this in its leaves and trust the wind to find your hands. If the blight fed on truth, I would starve it.

He stopped. Around him the camp continued its staccato of preparation. Somewhere to his right, Genn swore when a lash-knot slipped; Lira swatted him on the shoulder and redid it with vicious efficiency.

> You told me in a dream that not all roots want the same sun. I don't know if that was you or my fear, but I believe you were right. I am trying to grow toward what light I can find. If you are in shadow, I will learn to see in shadow. If you are angry, I will not ask you to be otherwise. If you are gone—

He lifted the charcoal. Bramble, as if called by the unspoken, nudged his elbow with a careful antler tip. "I know," Derwin murmured. He folded the scrap and slid it beneath the thong that held the dagger's sheath.

They met at dusk under the ragged canopy of the old gathering tree, now more scaffold than shelter. Joram represented the fighters; Kesa the healers and the elders; a trio of foragers had maps no one could trust but everyone needed; two mothers had the kind of clear-boned attention that made discussion sharper.

"The crow's mark to the north is broken," a forager said, tapping a charcoal map that stank of old tallow. "But new totems are going up farther east. They're not just staking roadways. They're drawing veins."

"Then we cut the veins," Joram said.

"Cut enough and you bleed the forest," Kesa countered. "We need to choose where to make the wound."

Derwin listened first. Old habit, hard-won. When the silence found him he leaned over the map and set a finger where three shallow streams met a stand of wind-bent pines. "Here," he said. "You can burn an artery with water."

"Water?" Joram's eyebrow lifted.

"The totems need purchase," Derwin said. "They're anchored in places where the soil is stubborn. But the water doesn't remember in the same way. Flood it. Shift it. Make the totem learn to breathe somewhere else while we take its breath."

Kesa's mouth tugged at one corner. "You want to make the land change its mind."

"I want to give it reason," Derwin said.

Plans accreted. Runners would test banks; two small teams would move at night with saws and silent wedges; no torches; no show of strength to tempt a drawn-out fight. Every choice was a gamble. But every gamble was better than waiting for the crow to choose the hour.

Before the light went fully, Derwin took the children to the perimeter where the earth rose in a low swell. The wind there smelled of iron and green. He knelt and drew a circle with the butt of his staff.

“This is not a spell,” he said. “It’s a promise.” He set a small seed in the dirt. “Not fruit. Not food. A witness.” He showed them the breath—the way his chest widened without lifting shoulders, the way his exhale fell into the soil like an apology. The seed trembled and did not sprout. Good. Let the lesson be honest.

“Sometimes,” he said, “the land needs only to know you would ask. It keeps the answer for later.”

Lira nodded, brow furrowed. Genn looked at the seed like it had insulted him. One of the smaller children, a girl with a missing tooth, whispered, “I’ll keep it a secret,” and cupped the tiny depression with both hands as if warming it.

Night widened its palms over the camp. Fires were kept low. The smell of stew thickened the air and thin bread blistered on hot stones. The children ate in clusters, legs tucked under them, shoulders touching. Derwin ate standing, leaning against Bramble as the beast watched the perimeter with that deceptively lazy alertness he trusted more than any man’s.

After bowls were rinsed and stacked, after the smallest were nudged toward sleep, the quiet work continued. Twine was doubled; sling-stones counted; signal horns tested with the softest of breaths. Kesa made her rounds with a bag of willow-bark and the kind of humor that kept people from boiling alive inside their own dread.

Marrec drifted at the edge of it all like a shadow that learned to wear a face. When he finally stepped into the firelight, Derwin felt the old split in his ribs tug.

"You'll be gone before dawn," Marrec said. Not a question.

"Yes."

"Good." A beat. "Bad." Another. "Fitting." He rubbed at his jaw. "I told Kesa we should never have let you stay. I was wrong about one part."

Derwin waited.

"You shouldn't have stayed this long," he said. "You should have been gone sooner. Doing this work. This is the only thing you're built for." He turned before Derwin could answer, his silhouette broken by the pale, raw trunk of a recent felled sapling.

When the moon tipped past its peak, Derwin walked the perimeter with Bramble. The beast placed each step as if choosing where to be born. Near the eastern notch in the earthwork, Bramble stopped, inhaled, and went still—so still the night seemed to settle around him.

"What do you hear?" Derwin asked, hand to the beast's neck.

Bramble did not answer, but the great head tilted, antlers tracing an invisible line northward. Derwin closed his eyes and leaned his thoughts into the silence the way he taught the children to lean their breath into root and water. For a sliver of a second—less—he felt it: a faint, arrhythmic thud. Not footsteps. Not hooves. Like two stones knocking together underwater. Totem heartbeats.

"We have until first light," Derwin murmured. Bramble's ear twitched in agreement.

Kesa gathered a handful of them for a brief rite under the old bough. No singing, no flame, nothing the blight might watch with too much attention. Just palms to earth and a word every person finished for themselves.

"Hold," she said, and they all said the rest—us. fast. brave. through.

When the circle loosened, she caught Derwin's sleeve. "The dagger," she said, voice even softer. "You've discovered what it is not."

"Not a weapon," he said.

"Only to the hand that chooses that truth," she answered. "To the other, it is precisely that. Keep choosing." She slipped a ribbon of bark into his palm. Etched there: a single spiral, barely visible. "For when words fail."

They ate again, because that is a kind of defiance. Genn burned the edges of three flatbreads and laughed so hard at his own failure he made two of the smaller children snort stew through their noses. Lira pretended to be furious and secretly tucked the blackest piece into her pouch "for luck."

"Not that kind," Derwin said.

"The only kind we can make," Lira countered.

He let her have that.

He spoke to no one about the dream of Ashling. Not yet. But as the camp thinned toward sleep he returned to the seed he set at the perimeter and touched two fingers to the soil. *I'm still asking,* he thought. *I'm still here.* The ground did not answer. Sometimes that is an answer.

He checked Bramble's tack. The saddle the children built had been improved in three small ways since he'd last inspected it—Lira's doing, surely. He tightened a strap, loosened another, then pressed his brow to Bramble's and let himself be held by the animal's enormous, living stillness.

The second watch belonged to Derwin. He paced a slow circuit, moving from shadow to shadow, listening for the wrong kind of silence. Twice he heard owls. Once a fox barked somewhere beyond the brook, the sound like laughter softened by cloth. He paused at the healer's lean-to. Kesa slept upright, chin to chest, pestle still in her hand. He draped a blanket over her shoulders and left the pestle there as a joke she would grumble at and keep.

The stars were good, though thin. He tried to read them and decided they were telling him only what he already knew: that the night makes everything feel farther away and nearer at once.

The camp woke as if roused by a single breath. Runners moved with those long, ground-eating strides that make no sound. Bread passed hand to hand. Water skins, sharpened pegs, coil upon coil of rope. Someone—one of the foragers—tucked fresh mint into Derwin's palm. "For the mouth," she said. "So you taste something living where it smells wrong."

He chewed, grateful. Joram shouldered a bundle of stakes and said, "If we die, we die after we finish this work." It was the closest he would come to tenderness.

Genn and Lira stood in front of Bramble like sentries denying a door to their own hearts.

Lira fixed a strap that did not need fixing.

Genn tried and failed to look taller.

"Back by tomorrow night," Derwin said, as if the forest took orders. "If I'm not, you know what to do."

He did not tell them what that was.

They did not ask.

He touched both their foreheads gently and, for once, without irony.

"Keep the rhythm."

They nodded—solemn, terrified, brave.

Bramble lowered himself beside the fire, curling in on his massive frame until he was a dark, breathing hill at the edge of the camp. The flames painted slow amber lines across his hide, then lost interest and sank.

The camp did not gather. No one made speeches. No one pretended this was anything other than what it was.

They had all learned to distrust the pageantry of farewells.

Derwin settled onto his bedroll, boots still on, pack within arm's reach. Sleep did not come. He did not expect it to.

Beyond the firelight, the forest whispered in unfamiliar rhythms.

Not loud enough to be language.
Not quiet enough to be ignored.

Derwin lay staring into the dark, feeling the camp around him—not as a place, but as a collection of names pressed like seeds into his palm. He closed his hand around them.
Tomorrow, he would ride.

Chapter Twenty Two

Dawn came thin and colorless, the sky the bruised underside of a river stone. The camp rose like a single animal, all breath and sinew and dull-eyed purpose. Derwin woke with the taste of iron behind his teeth and the dream of the Heart Tree still pricking his skin like frost. Bramble's bulk pressed warm against his shoulder—a mountain that had chosen to walk beside him—and for a precious heartbeat Derwin let himself be small.

"Hold," he whispered, palm to fur. The beast exhaled, slow and steady, the answer of old hills.

Kesa's shadow fell across Derwin's face. "Up," she said. "Before the forest decides without us." She tossed a strip of dried nettle-bread and two bitter berries onto his chest. "Chew both. I want you angry and awake."

He ate standing. Outside, the settlement had shut its fear into knots and lashings. Stakes bristled along the northern swell. Totem shards hung from cords like broken teeth, proof that the crow's network could bleed. Children with bandaged wrists carried water as solemnly as priests. Joram moved among the fighters like a blade made of orders. Lira and Genn checked sling stones, shared a glance that carried a whole childhood of bravery and lies.

Bramble nudged his spine. Now? the touch asked.

"Soon," Derwin murmured. And to himself, a quieter, "Forgive me if 'soon' becomes 'too late'."

They stood beneath the ragged canopy of the old gathering tree, a skeleton against the washed-out sky. The air had the clean, metallic taste that comes before lightning. Kesa pressed two green vials into Derwin's hand and tied the pouch shut with a knot he could free even while bleeding.

"I will ration these for you at a distance," she said. "Which is to say: don't die where I can't reach you."

Derwin tried to smile. "You've never asked for easy work."

"I asked once," she said. "The forest said no." Her gaze softened at the edges. "Listen for it anyway."

Joram approached with a roll of charcoal-stained bark. "Veins to the east and north," he said, pointing. "We break the eastern line at the pines first. Short route. Better footing. If they press, fall back to the river bend and flood the bank." He looked at Derwin's hands. "You steady?"

"I am what I am."

"Useful enough," Joram said, and left before sentiment had a chance to form.

The camp thinned, as if pulled forward by an invisible rope. Derwin knelt and dug two fingers into the earth. The soil was damp and cold, the heartbeat under it too fast.

"Be with me," he whispered. "Or bear witness." He would accept either.

Bramble knelt to be saddled. The children's work had been refined again—Lira's neat lashes, Genn's idiot-strong knots. Derwin swung up and settled into the familiar sway. Across the clearing, Lira lifted two fingers in a salute that meant more than love and less than goodbye; Genn mouthed, *don't be stupid*, meaning be stupid if we need you to.

Derwin breathed, once, twice. Bramble surged forward.

The eastern pines stood angled like ribs around a raw lung of earth. Mist clung to the needles, each droplet a bead of glass. Between the trunks, the first wave moved—shapes wrong in the way badly healed bones are wrong. Blighted deer lurched forward on split hooves packed with gray rot, flesh pulling away from bone in wet ribbons. Boars pushed through the brush with ribs showing beneath translucent skin, their bristles smoldering as if each hair remembered fire. Foxes skittered low to the ground, spines kinked at impossible angles, eyes glowing like coals buried under ash. Some animals wore too many joints. Some wore too few. All of them moved as if something else walked inside their hides.

"Hold the line," Joram called, his voice flint on stone. "Let them spend themselves."

Frontliners locked scavenged shields together—planks, hide-wrapped doors, cracked bucklers—anything wide enough to turn teeth and horn. The line shrank inward, becoming a wall with breath behind it.

Derwin slid from Bramble's back, every old injury waking to take attendance. He set his staff and planted his feet in the way Kesa taught when everything in him had been lighter. "Spiral," he told the first rank, and the staves answered: whirr, crack, redirect. The animals
struck like waves that could not remember how to turn.

Derwin breathed out and let his magic uncoil—not a surge, not a blaze, but the steady exhale of a patient fire. The ground answered with vines slick as river-rope, catching legs, easing momentum sideways, not to break but to spare. He didn't want to kill what had once belonged.

A boar hit his knee and spun him. The world tilted. Bramble slammed past him, antlers taking the beast mid-shoulder, a sound like a tree snapping under snow. Derwin found his feet and his breath at once. A fox skittered close, halted, stared at him with that torn, pleading stillness he had seen in the woods two nights before.

"I know," he said, low, and sent a thin, bright thread of will into the space between its ribs where the sickness hummed. The thread held; the hum faltered; the fox jerked like a puppet with one string cut and fled.

"Derwin," Joram snapped, "with me."

They shifted right as one, catching a surge before it rippled down the line. Lira's sling sang; A gray-cloaked druid drove a spear haft into Genn's wrist. He swore without losing grip. The camp did not break. It bent like willow and sprang back.

The second wave came with voices.

Hoods in gray bark-leather. Hands marked in soot spirals. The dark druids did not shout. They spoke the land's tongue and asked it to forget itself. Their totems pulsed on the edges of sight—bone-thorn, feather knots, stones drilled and threaded on gut.

Derwin tasted bile. "Cut the cords," he said. "Not the wood." He moved through the first knot, fingers quick, blade quicker: cut, twist, break the logic. The totems guttered like candles in wind.

A woman in a crow-feather mantle looked up at him through a curtain of hair. "Traitor to your soil," she said mildly, and called the root beneath his feet to turn.

It didn't.

His body remembered before his mind did: immune. Not a wall, but an unkind mirror the blight could not read. Her surprise cost her a breath. He wrapped the totem's thread around his palm and wrenched. The field stuttered. Three blighted deer staggered as if waking from fever.

"Push," Joram barked. "To the pines!"

They pushed. The first break opened like a mouth.

Kesa's hands had learned to move without asking permission from her joints. She stitched, bound, poured, cursed. The wounded came in a tide, then ebbed, then came again with different colors of blood. She sent a boy back to the line with willow bark and a lie—"You will be fine"—because sometimes mercy was the same shape as falsehood.

When the ground shivered under her stool she did not look up. She pressed a leaf to a woman's temple and whispered the breath that eased pain. Only when all three of her kettles rattled did she step outside and stare east.

The pines were shaking the way a body shakes as fever breaks.

"Hold," she said to no one. "Hold, you stubborn child." She did not know if she meant the forest or Derwin.

The crow let himself be seen when it would cost the most to see him. He stood on the low rise beyond the pines, staff black as burned wet bone, surrounded by a moving geometry of ash and feather. The air around him bent—a heat mirage made of cold thought. He smiled with only one side of his mouth.

"Derwin," he called, as if in greeting across a river. "Such a fine habit you have of arriving late."

Derwin felt the old guilt try to stand up inside him. He did not let it. “Your totems are clumsy.”

“My apprentices are eager,” the crow said. “They will learn by breaking. All good things do.” He gestured lazily. The ground in front of Derwin tore like wet cloth. From the rent crawled a thing that had once been a stag and now remembered only antler and hunger.

Bramble drove into it with his whole life. Derwin moved with the surge, rib shouting, shoulder numb. He struck low and bound a leg with grass that remembered how to be rope; he whispered to the soil until it forgot which way was up. Around him, the line screamed and sang and kept its feet.

Past the stag, beyond the press, Ashling walked into view.

She wore a half-mantle of dark leaves lacquered to shine like beetle wings. A mask rested on her brow, ready to fall. Her staff was not like his staff; it was longer, thinner, its runes cut like questions that had been asked too late. She did not look at Derwin. She looked at the camp with the detached curiosity of a child studying ants.

“Ashling,” he said before he could stop the word.

Her gaze flicked once, as if a moth had brushed her cheek. Then she lifted her hand and the field shifted: blight-creatures turned with machine grace, druids fanned to new positions, totems pivoted on lines Derwin hadn’t yet seen. She was not the crow’s echo.

She was a new voice in a chorus he’d thought he knew.

“Hold the fold!” Joram’s shout cracked like ice. Derwin tore his eyes away. He worked. He broke two more totems, cut three cords, dragged a man from the mire pretending to be earth. He lost the count of cuts and breaths. Somewhere in the scar of the day, Genn stumbled and Lira dragged him up by the collar and hit him, and he laughed blood onto her sleeve and kept moving.

The crow's voice carried again, intimate as a whisper under a door. "Walk to her, Derwin. Or do you need the children to go first?"

Derwin bared his teeth. "You talk because you are afraid to listen." He pulled a charm from his pouch, the bark spiral Kesa had pressed on him, and snapped it in his fist. Something in the air around the crow's left-hand totems hiccupped. Four cords went slack. Five men breathed easier.

The crow finally frowned. "Interesting." He raised his staff.

The sky went black with birds.

They were not crows. They were everything the forest could make with a wing when cruel hands taught it to forget. Beetle-feathered, bone-sparred, eyes like polished seeds carved out of winter. They fell like rain.

"Under!" Derwin shouted. Shields slammed up along the front rank, cloaks whipped overhead. Bramble reared and took three from the air with antlers and jaw. Derwin grabbed a boy and rolled with him as the birds tore into leather and hair. One caught Derwin's cheek and left fire in its wake.

"Up!" Joram again. Always Joram. They stood. The birds wheeled and fell and wheeled again until the crow's staff dipped and they became what birds become when the moment has passed: frantic, hungry, mortal.

The press eased. The press returned.

Time lost meaning and turned into noise.

"Left!" Lira shouted, and Genn threw without looking. The sling stone cracked a totem square, not enough to break it, but it made the field forget itself long enough for three bodies to get through. Genn's wrist ached in a clean, righteous way.

"That's seven," he panted.

"That's three," Lira said. "Count true, idiot." She shoved him behind a brace and took his place under a rain of ash.

They moved as the camp moved: toward Derwin when he surged; away from him when the line needed a hinge. Lira's hair was a dark rope down her back, her face streaked and alight. Genn's eyes shone like someone who finally found the right sort of trouble.

"Do you think he can save her?" Genn asked, as if words were coins he could spare.

"No," Lira said, and then, softer, "Yes."

It was not a decision. It was a remembering. Derwin saw Ashling across a churned expanse where the blight had tried to write a new language in mud, and he began to walk.

"Derwin!" Joram barked.

"I'll be back," Derwin said, and believed it the way a seed believes in spring. He walked.

The battle did not stop for him. He did not stop for it. Things struck and were deflected by old practice and by luck and by Bramble, who paced to his right with the kind of calm that makes predators choose new prey. Arrows thudded into earth near his boots, hissed past his cheek. A dark druid reached for Derwin's staff and found instead the calm backhand of a tired man who had no more patience to spare for boys who wanted to be monsters.

Through it all, the forest's breath rose and fell, hot with panic and then, strangely, cool. A path opened where no path should have been; a thicket leaned aside; a root slid like a snake under his sole to keep him from a pit. He was not the forest's favorite son. But today, the forest did not want to see him fall.

Ashling turned when he'd closed half the distance. Mask down now. Her eyes were twin wells under leaf-shadow.

"Derwin," she said, voice perfect and flat. "You are late."

"I have been late my whole life," he answered. "I'm trying to arrive."

She did not smile. "You left me to burn."

"I left you to live."

Something passed over her features like a cloud moving across a pond—shadow that becomes reflection becomes light becomes shadow again. "You taught me the forest forgives," she said. "You lied."

"The forest remembers," he said. "Forgiveness is something we do with remembering, or else it isn't forgiveness at all."

She lifted her staff. The air around her trembled like a plucked string. "He says you'll say pretty things," she murmured. "He says you will try to make me a child again."

The crow appeared to her left, a correction in the symmetry.

“Ask him where he went those nights,” he told her conversationally. “Ask him what he chose when the choice was you or his pride.”

Derwin tasted the temptation, rich and poisonous: to argue with the crow instead of speaking to Ashling. He kept his eyes on her. “I chose fear,” he said. “And I chose you when I remembered I could.” He set the dagger’s sheath on his belt like an offering that could cut. “I am not asking you to forgive me. I am asking you to walk with me again.”

“Walk where?” she asked. “Into your apology?”

“Into the place where you don’t have to listen to him,” Derwin said. “Into the place where the blight is a thing we fight, not a thing we are.”

The crow’s voice was all silk. “Strike him,” he crooned. “Show him you have learned.”

Ashling’s hand tightened. Derwin saw the small tremor in her wrist that said sleep had not visited her well. He stepped closer. Bramble rumbled—and stopped when Derwin lifted a palm.

“Ashling,” Derwin said, and let his voice be the voice he had used in the circle, in the quiet mornings, over bad tea and good bread. “I promised you once that I would not leave you behind again. I am here to keep that promise. Even if you send me away.”

The tremor stilled. For an instant her shoulders loosened, her chin lifted in the old, defiant angle that meant she was listening even when she refused to say so.

Then the crow turned his staff a fraction and the air behind Ashling filled with a sound like children calling a name that had never been theirs. She flinched as if struck. He had learned her ghosts.

“Stop,” Derwin said to the crow, not as a plea but as a command.

The crow only smiled.

Ashling struck.

It was not a killing blow. It was an ending blow—a bright, terrible wave that tore up the ground between them and hammered him back through ten years of mistakes. Bramble hurled himself sideways and absorbed half of it, antlers blackening at the tips, fur smoking. Derwin hit earth hard enough to see white.

He rolled, breath clawing at his ribs, and came up on one knee, staff planted, dagger ready in his other hand. Ashling was already stepping back, face bare now and stricken—not with pity but with the rigid misery of someone who has done exactly what she knew she would do.

“Go,” the crow said, gentle as a lullaby. “Take what you’ve learned and leave this gutter.”

Ashling glanced at Derwin. In that one look was every lesson they had ever shared and every silence between them. She shook her head once, infinitesimal, at him or herself or the world, and turned away.

“Wait,” Derwin said, not as a command this time but as a prayer.

She did not.

They withdrew, the crow with the slow, insulting calm of

someone who has never had to run, Ashling walking as if the ground would swallow her if she rushed it.

Kesa reached Derwin at a dead run she had not attempted since she'd been a different kind of woman. She slammed the heel of her hand into his sternum and snarled, "Breathe." When he did she poured one of the green vials between his teeth and dared him with her eyes to choke. "You don't get to die of something as boring as air." She turned and laced a line of children's forearms with willow bark and stolen courage. "You—left flank. You—keep the small ones behind Bramble's shadow. You—cry later." She swayed once, from knee to hip, the way old trees sway in a high wind. "Spirits take me for caring," she muttered, and went to find another wound to bully shut.

"Derwin!" Joram's voice, ragged as torn bark. "Now!"

He stood on legs that remembered how, and what had been a personal grief widened to become a field again. The press surged toward the gap Ashling's blast had carved. Derwin lifted his staff and his voice at once.

"Hold," he said, and the line held. "Left hinge forward! Right coil! Bramble—down!"

Bramble dropped his head and pushed a river of bodies back a step, then two blight-things poured into the opening—wolves whose jaws hung by threads, a bear dragging its own hindquarters, birds crawling instead of flying with wings bent the wrong way. The ground squelched under the weight of rot. The air filled with a copper-sweet stench that burned the back of the throat.

Genn and Lira appeared at Derwin's flanks like the memory of better days. He could taste the shape of the battle now: where it could be bent, where it could not. He moved where his absence would cost lives, not where his presence would win praise.

The field learned him. He learned it back.

What followed felt like a week packed into an hour: assault, recoil, adjust; wedge, turn, seal; the crow probing, withdrawing, laughing soft at the wrong places. Derwin burned three totems, drowned two in their own logic, learned to hear where the cords hummed beneath the ground. He set his palm to the earth and asked without demanding and the earth, exhausted, said yes twice and no once, and the no was as holy as the yes.

They took the pines back by inches. They left a trail of names they would speak later. Bramble bled from a dozen small cuts and stood as if carved there by the first wind. Genn's sling went slack when his shoulder failed; Lira traded him a staff without breaking rhythm and swore she would lash his arm back on with sinew if he dropped it.

At last the crow pulled his people back with two economical gestures. The field sighed. The birds rose like smoke and became sky again. The quiet that fell was not peace. It was the shock after a bone slides home.

Derwin stood in a circle of ground that had turned from black to gray to brown.

He could feel the place remembering itself.

He could feel the gap where Ashling had chosen not to stand.

They counted. They carried. They dug. No fire—Kesa forbade it until the land had more breath. The wounded made those low, animal sounds that stop when a hand is held. The dead lay with their mouths closed and their eyes not quite so.

Derwin moved through it like a man walking inside a bell that had just been struck. He said small things that meant I see you and I am here and I am sorry without using any of those words. He touched Bramble's singed fur and felt the beast's answering huff in his own ribs.

At the edge of the reclaiming, where the soil had lifted its head but not yet stood, he sank to one knee. He drew the dagger from its sheath and set it on the ground, point toward him, hilt toward the horizon. Light collected on the blade and did not choose a side.

"I will plant," he said, to Kesa when she came to stand beside him, to the children who hovered at a distance, to the ghosts who had good aim with their stones. "Not tonight. But soon."

Kesa nodded, the tired pride of a person whose heart had been right and wrong so many times she no longer kept score. "You will plant," she said. "And you will fail. And you will plant again."

He looked to the trees where Ashling had vanished. The branches there hadn't settled yet; they trembled like mouths that had spoken too much truth.

"Not all roots want the same sun," he said.

"Some learn," Kesa answered.

He closed his hand around the hilt of the dagger and felt it become, briefly, a promise rather than a threat.

The camp lay down in shifts and dreamed the kinds of dreams that eat holes in blankets. Derwin did not sleep. He walked the limit of what they reclaimed until dawn's first thin blade cut the eastern sky again. In the place where Ashling had stood he found a single leaf from her lacquered mantle, black-green and beautiful and wrong.

He folded it like a prayer and put it in the pouch with the letter he would never send.

Then he went to find a seed.

Chapter Twenty Three

The quiet came first.

Not peace—never that simple—but a hollow stillness laid over the forest like the skin on cooled broth. The after-silence of thunder. It held the shapes of things that had happened: broken branches, churned earth, ash still drifting in hesitant flakes. It held breath; it did not yet exhale.

Derwin stood on the ridge where the battle had broken and then broken again. Mud clung to his boots like need. In the distance, wisps of smoke threaded from the blight pyres, thin and bitter. The air smelled of iron and doused flame. Beneath it, barely there, a cleaner scent waited—wet bark, river stone, rain that had not yet fallen.

Bramble came up beside him and leaned, scratched and singed and uncomplaining, simply being there the way mountains are there whether or not the sky remembers them. Derwin laid a hand against his neck and felt the slow, stubborn pulse—answering, anchoring.

Below, the survivors moved in murmurs and knots. No cheering; no triumph. The work after a near-ending never looked like celebration. Genn hauled a broken barricade to the side with one good shoulder and made a joke that cost him a wince. Lira laughed despite herself, then wheeled and helped Kesa lift a boy whose leg had turned the wrong color from a glancing curse. Joram stalked the perimeter, swapping commands for water skins, fury for lists.

Derwin let himself watch for a full minute longer, a greedy minute he could never quite afford. Then he slid down the ridge, each step breaking the crust so the earth could remember how to take a footprint again. His ribs counted their objections. His shoulder rehearsed new limits. He welcomed each complaint like a census of what he still had.

Kesa met him at the edge of the clearing. Old griefs had carved fine rivers down her face, and now sweat traced them new. She did not embrace him. She placed two fingers on his sternum like setting a stone in a cairn and said simply, “Time.”

Derwin nodded. He didn’t ask for what. His hand had already found the small pouch against his ribs—the seed, warm as a kept truth.

They cleared a space where the ground had softened from black to reluctant brown. No rune-work. No fanfare. The circle formed out of tired bodies who remembered how to stand together. Even the wounded were wheeled or carried to the edge; even the children were quiet without being told.

Bramble folded himself behind Derwin like a stone lintel.

He knelt.

The seed looked like nothing at all—an ovoid of pale wood, grain swirled tight as a fingertip’s whorl. If you didn’t know what it was, you’d have called it an acorn’s shy cousin. Derwin held it in his palm and felt only a patient expectancy, not hunger. He thought of the first lesson he had taught in the old grove—the way Ashling’s hands trembled over the soil and how he told her the land listens, if you do.

He pressed the seed into the earth. The ground, still bruised, accepted it with a small, clean sound.

From the other pouch he drew the vial—liquid light caught like dawn in glass. His fingers hesitated. Not from doubt. From gravity. He tipped, and the drop fell.

Light traveled in the thin bright filaments one sees in old wood when it's split clean—the veins of a life remembering itself. Gold runnels raced outward, hesitated at knots of tainted soil, then pushed through like roots finding cracks in stone. A breeze lifted from nowhere and held. People breathed the same breath without meaning to.

The light pulsed once at the circle's edge and then sank, modest as a promise kept quietly.

The seed did not sprout. It did not need to perform for them.

But the air lost its flinch.

Kesa's voice came after the silence had proven it could hold. "Witness," she said, quiet but undeniable, and the word ran around the ring like warm rain.

Derwin stood slowly. His knees popped and made small liars of him.

Kesa stepped forward. She hadn't washed the blood off her hands; it dried into the lines like an old map. "This grove does not knight people," she said dryly. "We don't have the hats for it. But we remember the shape of a thing we can trust." Her gaze moved to Derwin and didn't waver. "You left because you thought staying would kill us. You returned when running would have been easier. You stood between children and a monster when the numbers were bad. You planted when it still hurt to kneel." She lifted one palm. "I name you Arch Druid, because a grove should have a heart that listens before it beats. Bear the name with humility and stubbornness in equal parts." A ghost of a smile passed over her mouth. "And sleep sometimes, or I'll knock you myself."

Murmurs rose—the steady assent of people who have no energy left for decoration. Joram's chin dipped once. Lira wiped her face with her wrist and succeeded only in moving the dirt around. Genn started to clap and, finding himself alone in the impulse, turned it into a vigorous rubbing of his hands, grinning like a boy caught stealing bread.

Derwin swallowed the heat in his throat. "I'll carry the name," he said, letting the words be simple so they could be true. "And I'll keep learning how. I'll protect the ones who cannot, and I'll teach the ones who can—until I'm a worse teacher than they are." He shifted a glance to the children on the rim. "Which won't be long."

A small ragged laugh made the circle breathe again.

The work resumed because the world did not stop to admire vows. Derwin moved with it, not above it. He splinted where he could, lifted where he should, stepped back where someone else knew better. Kesa barked him into drinking water, then barked him into drinking more.

At the first pyre, they laid wild bodies on wild wood. Not as trophy. As apology. Lira asked for a word; Kesa nodded at Derwin. He bent and set his palm to a fallen stag's brow. In the contact he felt flickers—memory not of what the creature had done, but of rain tasted, of frost on whisker, of a ditch that smelled of old leaves. The blight had not owned those things. It had only worn the body for a while.

"Go," he said softly, and the word had the shape of thank you inside it. Flame took.

At the second pyre, Genn pulled a bead-string from his pocket—

scraps of wood with children's names carved in the shaky hand of someone who had practiced letters with a knife. He knelt and showed it to Derwin like a confession. "They gave them to me," he said. "The people we met on the road. The ones who—" He didn't finish the sentence. "So we'd carry the names to the trees."

"We will," Derwin said. "All the way." He did not ask to hold the string. He did not need to be the pair of hands for every burden. He just stood there so Genn didn't have to hold it alone.

By the river bend, a woman sat with her back to a rock, hands loose and empty on her knees. Derwin crouched in front of her. "Who?" he asked gently, because sometimes it is easier to say a name when someone else makes room for it.

"My sister," the woman said without looking up. "She always braided my hair before market. Even when we hated each other." A broken sound escaped her. "She would have hated this."

"Let me hate it with you," Derwin said. They did, for a while, in the dry way of people who have outcried themselves.

When the worst of the lifting was done, Kesa claimed an hour with him the way a blacksmith claims a blade—without asking it how it feels about being tempered. She dragged him to the healer's tarp and made him sit on a crate that had seen better uses. Bramble sank like a dropped hill outside the flap and started snoring without shame.

Kesa cleaned his cheek where a bird had tried to take a bite of his face. The salve burned like honesty. "Turn," she said, and prodded a bruise that looked like a map of the eastern pines.

"You could say please," Derwin muttered.

"I could also say stop bleeding and see which one you manage," she replied. "Lift your arm."

He did. The motion lit a row of small fires along his ribs. He let them burn. "You were right," he said after a bit. "About planting even when it hurts."

"I am wrong about most things loudly," Kesa said. "But I will be right quietly about this: you are allowed to be tired." She set a firm hand on his shoulder until the tremor acknowledged it was seen and therefore had to behave. "You do not save anyone by turning into a story."

He breathed, shaky and grateful. "I wrote her a letter," he said, surprising himself. "I never gave it."

"Then write another," Kesa said. "That's what letters are for. Failing. Trying again. The forest keeps no copies."

He almost laughed. "What if she doesn't read it?"

Kesa bandaged the last cut like she was tying up a loose argument. "Then you will have said it to yourself. That is often the harder audience." She straightened, bones popping in a sympathetic chorus. "Eat. Sleep. Pretend for a few hours that the world can turn without you. Then wake, and be a fool for it again."

He bowed his head, a small child's gesture he did not mind being seen making.

Derwin found Genn and Lira near the half-mended palisade sharing a stolen heel of bread and the sort of look you only exchange after both nearly dying and nearly laughing at it. He sat without asking and held out what remained of a tart someone had thrust at him without explanation. They tore it three ways and pretended not to notice that Bramble's sleeping bulk had migrated close enough to count as a wall.

"You walked through a battlefield like it was a hallway," Genn announced between heroic chews. "Terrible role model."

"I tripped twice," Derwin said.

"Did not see," Lira lied. She nudged his boot with hers. "Did she—" She stopped. Refused to make him answer the kind of question that can only hurt.

"She left," he said. Honesty sat better than explanation. "We will see her again." He didn't add not knowing in which direction she'd be walking.

Genn leaned back on his hands and stared up at a patch of sky that had rediscovered the color blue. "If you are Arch Druid now," he said, "does that mean your rules are law? Because I have notes."

"Submit in triplicate," Derwin joked.

"We don't have triplicate," Genn said, outraged.

Lira smiled without showing teeth. "We have charcoal and two sticks."

"Then it is decided," Derwin said gravely. "We will invent paperwork. The grove will perish of tedium."

Lira's smile faltered into thought. "You cleansed that fox by the ravine, the night before the river bend. I saw enough to know it wasn't luck."

"I… touched a place in it that wasn't sick," Derwin said. The words came slow, like feeling for a path with bare feet. "Or maybe it touched a place in me that couldn't be."

"And you think you can teach it," Genn said, not as challenge, as anticipation.

"I think I can try." He looked at them both—their young intensity, their old scars. "Not yet. But soon. We'll start with listening. Then with small, patient things."

Lira nodded like a soldier taking a post. "We'll be there."

"You'll regret it," Derwin said.

"Probably," Genn said cheerfully.

Evening gave way to a night that did not press. The stars came out shyly and then with more courage, until the sky remembered its own work. Derwin walked the boundary of the reclaimed ground with a slow pace and bare hands. He let his fingers trail the tops of grasses that dared stand again. He touched stones that warmed under innocent suns before any tree had been asked to choose sides.

At the far edge, a ribbon of water threaded quiet as thought. He knelt and cupped it and drank. Cold seeped into his gums, into old hurts, into the worry that hardened without him noticing. When he looked up, he saw a fox on the opposite bank. Not the one from the ravine, perhaps. Or perhaps exactly so. It watched him without fear and then went about its business—sniffing, stepping, leaving the earth better for the pressure of its paws.

Derwin sat there a long time, listening to the place learn how to breathe again. Every now and then the wind brought him a sound that didn't belong—the far scrape of something building where it should only unbuild. He did not follow the sound with his feet.

He followed it with the map in his head. He made a small cross where it would keep until morning.

When he returned to camp, a quiet had settled that did not feel like absence. People slept in twos and threes; Bramble slept like a continent. Kesa dozed upright against a post because she was the kind of creature that forgot to put herself down. Derwin draped a blanket over her and did not mention it later.

He lay on his back and stared up through the ribs of a shelter whose roof had not yet been replaced. The stars arranged themselves into a pattern that meant nothing and therefore everything. He closed his eyes, and for the first time in too long, sleep came when called.

He woke before dawn. Dreams had visited, but they kept their knives out of his ribs. He found a quiet corner by the gathering tree, dug a charcoal stick from his pouch, and tore a scrap from a sack that had failed as a sack but would succeed as paper.

He wrote without preface:

> Ashling—
>
> The day I left, I said I was going to look for help. That was true and also a lie. I was looking for a way to be the person you needed without being the person I was. It turns out there is no road for that. There is only walking the one under your feet and not leaving the people on it.
>
> I have learned how to stand still in front of a moving thing. I have learned how to plant a seed even when I don't believe in spring. I have learned that promises are not spells. They are gardens. You can't speak one and then go inside and expect it to water itself.

I am Arch Druid now because people keep insisting I am something I have not finished becoming. I don't know what to do with that except keep becoming. If you read this one day, I hope you are not reading it as a prisoner of a voice that uses your scars as reins. I hope you are reading it to laugh at how serious I am. I hope you are angry at me in the way that means you still expect something from me.

I planted the seed today. The land took it. It didn't make a miracle for us. It only accepted. That is enough for a first morning.

I will not stop looking for you. Not to drag you. To walk alongside you, or behind you, or to wait where the path is safe until you want to sit in shade.

You once asked if the forest forgives. I don't know. But I do. And I am trying to deserve yours.

—D.

He folded the scrap and slid it into the pouch with the bead-string and the leaf from her lacquered mantle. The pouch had become a reliquary of things not yet finished.

Midmorning brought a ceremony only because the children refused to let the day pass without one. They strung white flowers on thin cords and draped them over Bramble, who bore the indignity with the long-suffering patience of a sainted ox. They chalked a spiral on Derwin's cheek and pretended it made him look wise. They held up their hands in an approximation of solemnity and shouted, all at once, "Don't be stupid!"—which, in their dialect, meant we love you, please don't die doing math with knives.

Kesa watched with an expression that, on anyone else, would have been a grin. "Good," she said. "Let his first orders be in a language he understands."

Derwin endured it gladly. He endured worse things for worse reasons. This felt like being heavy in the right direction.

After, Joram brought him a roll of bark with a map's bones sketched in charcoal—the new lines of defense, the places where the land still hummed wrong, the cut points for the cord network that would try to regrow. They bent their heads and argued quietly about sensible things: numbers, distances, sleep rotations. It felt like mercy to speak in details.

At dusk, the circle returned of its own accord. They brought water and silent toasts and a fiddle that had lost two strings but remembered three. Someone hummed an old planting song; someone else built a harmony and then forgot it, which is its own kind of music. The seed did not stir, but if one stood very still, they could imagine the whisper of cambium thinking about its first task.

Derwin walked the outer rim while the others rested inside it. He stopped at each compass point and touched the ground and said the names he had been given to carry on the bead-string. He did not make them magic. He made them heard. The forest has its own theology about that kind of thing.

When he completed the circle, Genn tossed him a dried apple slice with the precision of a boy who had learned to turn mischief into aim. Lira passed him a small clay cup of something that remembered being wine. Kesa tipped her chin at the seed and said, "You realize you have to grow with it. Annoying, I know."

“Terrible,” Derwin said. “Do you suppose there’s a way to outsource maturity?”

“Children,” Kesa said. “They will loan you theirs if you ask nicely.”

Derwin looked at the ring of faces—smeared, lined, lit from within by the sort of stubbornness that keeps a place on the map. “I will ask,” he said.

Night thickened again, kinder than the last. In the small hours, Derwin woke and padded barefoot to the circle. The ground kept a hint of the day’s warmth, like a kettle remembering tea. He knelt where he pressed the seed and set both hands flat.

He did not ask for anything. He reported. Like a child to a tree that had always been taller than the house, he told the land what they had done and what they had broken and what they had mended poorly with twine and will. He told it about Ashling in a voice that did not demand a verdict. He told it about the fox that had gone about its business.

At the edge of hearing, at the edge of bone, something answered. Not words. The sensation of a door opening and finding a room you had always owned but never entered. The faintest sense of sap rising.

Derwin bowed his head. “Thank you,” he said, and meant for bearing witness more than for helping. He would take either. He would take both and not pretend to deserve them.

He woke to a sky rinsed clean. Birds tried two notes and then committed to a third. The air had the taste the world gets after crying—a clarity that hurts and heals at once. Derwin stretched and succeeded at all but three of his usual joints. Bramble yawned a canyon’s worth of tooth and regarded him with the patient fondness of something that had survived.

There were plans to make. There were letters to send to places that did not yet know they were connected to this one. There were wounded to move to gentler shade and fences to stitch where blight liked to cheat. There was a totem in the west that had learned to hide under river stones; Joram's map had sworn at it in three different inks. There was bread to bake and new stories to tell wrong on purpose so the children could heckle him into telling them right.

There was also—quiet as a splinter—the knowledge that the blight did not end because one field had remembered its name. In the far treeline a branch shifted though no wind took it. A rhythm pulsed too steady to be bird wing. Somewhere, the crow would be setting new cords. Somewhere, Ashling would be looking at a seed of her own and arguing with it.

Derwin stood at the circle's edge and looked down at the unassuming mound that held more future than seemed polite. He thought of Kesa's admonition: *grow with it*. He thought of the letter in his pouch and the leaf and the beads of names worn smooth by thumb.

He touched the ground. "We'll meet you where you are," he told the world—not as prophecy, as decision. "And we'll keep coming back."

Behind him, camp noises resumed—the bright clack of cups, the dull music of hammer on stake, a child's triumphant cheer over a beetle discovered and spared. Bramble rose and shook, shedding a constellation of dried petals from last night's garland. Lira called for Derwin to come learn a new knot she'd invented just to annoy him. Genn shouted that he'd invented a game where paperwork exploded.

Derwin smiled and stepped into the day.

The seed did not stir.

It didn't have to. It was already at work.

And so were they.

David A. Royster

I am a storyteller who has always felt the world most clearly through imagination — not as an escape, but as a way to witness and repair what is broken. Growing up, I was drawn to the kind of stories where wonder walked alongside grief: *Treasure Planet*, *Atlantis*, *Hercules, Percy Jackson* — tales where flawed heroes stumble toward growth, where loss leaves scars, but where light is still worth carrying forward. Those stories taught me that hope is not naive; it's hard-won. That same lesson shapes everything I write.

The Grove Beneath the Ash, my debut fantasy novel, is the most personal work I've written. At its heart, it reflects my own journey: carrying the weight of legacy, learning to trust in my chosen family, and discovering that survival is not enough if it isn't paired with belonging. Derwin, my protagonist, is a druid who believes he is broken by his past, but who learns that the very scars he carries can become the tools to protect and heal others. In many ways, his path mirrors my own desire to take pain, loss, and silence and turn them into something that breathes new life into the world.

I live in Southern California with my wife, my first and fiercest supporter. We grew up together, and her steady presence has been the anchor that allowed me to pursue writing as more than a dream. When I'm not writing or running games, I am exploring music, worldbuilding projects, and other creative pursuits that keep me close to that original spark — the belief that stories can change the way we see ourselves, and give us the courage to keep going.

www.ingramcontent.com/pod-product-compliance
Lightning Source LLC
LaVergne TN
LVHW100524110826
845146LV00002B/769

* 9 7 9 8 9 9 0 8 3 9 6 9 4 *